The Book of Names

A collection of mysterious tales

Richard Storry

By the same author

The Cryptic Lines
The Enigma of Heston Grange
Order of Merit
The Black Talisman
The Virtual Lives of Godfrey Plunkett

The Ruritanian Rogues Saga:
Volume I: A Looming of Vultures
Volume II: A Nest of Vipers
Volume III: A Shroud of Darkness
Volume IV: A Betrayal of Trust
Volume V: A Hoard of Treasures
Volume VI: A Conflict of Loyalties

Cover design: Gergö Pocsai

All titles are available from www.crypticpublications.com in paperback, in audio format and as downloads for e-readers.

ISBN: 9798642393512

Close the door. Write with no one looking over your shoulder. Don't try to figure out what other people want to hear from you; figure out what you have to say. It's the one and only thing you have to offer.
                                                            —*Barbara Kingsolver*

The Book of Names

A collection of mysterious tales

Contents

Alice..1

Frank 27

Greta...39

Frederick & Neville...47

Cora 60

David...74

Edith..92

Gerald..94

Martha 111

Owen.. 121

Ricarda & Samuel.. 138

Alice

"Oh, do come along, Alice! Do you want me to miss the boat?"

"Of course not, Ma'am. I'm very sorry."

Lady Olga Parchenko strode purposefully along the jetty towards the impressive craft, with its queue of people waiting to board, while her breathless maidservant struggled along behind, laden down with far more luggage than one person could realistically carry.

Several steamers made up the fleet which plied their trade on Lake Windermere, including *Swift, Swan* and *Teal*. Operating in rotation, these ships would ferry excited tourists up and down the picturesque strip of water throughout the year. So popular were these lake cruises that people flocked to them, even when the weather was drab and grey, and much of the beautiful scenery was shrouded in mist. However, when the skies were clear and the sun was shining, the hills and forests were seen at their resplendent best, creating an atmosphere which was both serene and relaxing.

Today was just such a day.

And, today, the craft securely moored along the jetty's

edge was *Tern,* the fleet's flagship. A short distance away, on the shore, a brass band was playing, while the multi-coloured bunting strung along the boat's railings and balustrades was fluttering in the light breeze, helping to create a real sense of occasion.

Upon reaching the pleasure boat, Lady Olga stopped and turned to look back at her maid, who was obliged to move quite slowly, due to being so heavily laden.

"When I agreed to offer you a position," she called, with a piercing voice which carried clearly to everyone nearby, "I had no idea you would be so slow. This tardiness is really not helping me at all. Once we're on board, I'll need you to bring me some tea. I'm absolutely parched, but you obviously don't care about that."

"I'm trying my best, Lady Olga," Alice gasped. "I'll be there in a moment."

"Quickly, then. Chop chop. Oh, for goodness sake, do get a move on. I've half a mind to instruct the captain to leave without you."

Lady Olga turned on her heal and, for the briefest of moments, addressed the orderly queue.

"Excuse me!" she ordered.

Then, ignoring the surprised stares from those who would soon become her fellow passengers, she pointedly stepped past them and onto the gangplank.

"Disgraceful behaviour!" muttered a retired colonel in the queue, whose monocle had fallen from his eye in astonishment at what he had just witnessed.

"Yes, who does she think she is?" said a young mother who was standing next to him, and trying her best to keep her two young children still while they waited to board.

"People like that think they own the place," said another woman. "Just 'cos they've got a bit of money they think they can do what they like and ride roughshod over everyone else."

As Olga Parchenko set foot on the deck, the captain and first officer were waiting, and both gave a smart salute.

"Welcome aboard, Lady Olga," said the captain, offering his hand.

The aristocrat ignored the polite welcome and swept past, looking around in all directions.

"And exactly where am I supposed to get some tea?" she asked, loudly, of no one in particular. "I thought I had a reservation."

The captain motioned to one of the stewards who quickly approached the wealthy Russian.

"If you'll come this way, my Lady," said the steward, "it will be my pleasure to escort you to our lounge, where an area has been set aside, especially for you."

Lady Olga paused, surveying this smartly attired member of the crew, and looking him up and down, before finally deciding, almost reluctantly, that he met with her approval.

"Very well," she said, "though I think you may need to arrange some assistance for my maid. She came highly recommended so I was persuaded to take her on – against my better judgement, I might add. I am sorry to say that so far she has shown herself to be quite, quite useless."

The steward nodded and, having indicated to another crew member to take care of Lady Olga, he swiftly traversed the gangplank, reaching the jetty just as the over-burdened maid arrived.

"Here, Miss," he said, "please let me help you with those."

"Oh, would you?" Alice replied. "That's really most kind."

As she tried to divest herself of the pile of packages and various items of luggage, they all suddenly slipped from her grasp and fell onto the jetty in a disorganised heap. At the same moment she stumbled and fell against the steward who, in turn, almost lost his balance too. For a moment, it looked as though they might be about to fall into the lake but, leaning on each other for support, they managed to regain their footing.

"I'm so sorry," she whispered, her shy eyes looking downwards.

"Not to worry, Miss," said the steward, releasing his grip on her arm and looking momentarily awkward. "You get on board and find your Mistress. I'll deal with this."

Alice gave half a nervous smile by way of thanks, and brushed a wisp of hair from her face.

"You come and stand over here with me, my dear," said the old colonel, from his place in the queue. "I'll look after you. We can get on board together. A young lady should never be treated like that."

"Thank you," said Alice, simply. Then, with another nod of appreciation to the steward, she left him to sort out the jumble of Lady Olga's possessions, while she slipped into the line alongside the colonel. A short while later, she finally succeeded in boarding the boat, where she received a welcoming smile from the captain – though there was no handshake for her.

***

Amongst those standing in the queue on the jetty, and still waiting to board, were a man and woman, both in their early thirties. Under her breath, the woman muttered.

"She shouldn't be allowed to get away with that sort of behaviour."

The man's eyebrows rose.

"What? What did you say?"

"I said…," the woman rolled her eyes in exasperation,

4

"that well-to-do woman thinks she can throw her weight around and lord it over everyone else, just because she's wealthy."

"Is it really that much of an issue for you?"

"Yes. Yes, it is, actually. You saw how rudely she spoke to her maid, and she was clearly not in the least concerned that all of us could hear what she said. It was embarrassing for the maid and embarrassing for us. On top of that, she then had the audacity to jump the queue and board the boat ahead of us."

"Calm yourself, my dear," said Scott. "You know the boat won't leave until we are all safely on board."

"But how are we supposed to do our job if we are to be kept standing here?"

"Your enthusiasm is commendable, but be patient, there's a good girl."

Diana gave an exasperated gasp.

"How exactly can we keep an eye on him if we're not on board?"

"We will be, very soon. In any case, you saw how he came running to help the maid with all that luggage. Did that look like someone who isn't trying his very best to fit back into society?"

"You clearly have more faith in human nature than I do."

The two detectives had been assigned to shadow the steward, whose name was Denny Wright, and who had recently been released from prison on parole. Having managed to persuade the parole board that he would no longer be a danger to anyone, his request for release had been granted, but he had been given a stern warning that his continued liberty was conditional upon good behaviour. It was the job of detectives Scott Jackson and Diana Law to ensure that the directive was being followed, though they were to do so discreetly, if possible.

***

At last, after all the passengers were finally aboard, the gangplank was removed and the large steamboat slowly pulled away from the jetty. In suitably majestic fashion, with the sound of the brass band still audible from the shore, and with the Lake District fells providing an elegant backdrop, she began to glide, smoothly and serenely, towards the deeper waters of Lake Windermere.

"This is your captain speaking," came a voice from the loudspeaker. "We would like to welcome you on board the *Tern*, which is the longest ship in the Windermere fleet. You've certainly come on a good day, with picture postcard weather, so the photographers amongst you will be able to take some wonderful photos as we make our way down the lake. You may notice we'll shortly be going past a narrow gap in the hills and, if you're quick, and especially eagle-eyed, you just might spot the famous landmark of Heston Grange in the distance. For now, though, relax and enjoy the journey, and do not hesitate to ask a member of the crew if there is anything we can do to make it more comfortable for you."

Inside the boat, at the far end of the sumptuous salon, curtains had been drawn across the windows, and a partitioning screen had been unfolded to provide a degree of privacy for Lady Olga.

"Wouldn't you like to see the scenery, Ma'am?" asked Alice, as she approached, skilfully stepping round the edge of the dividing screen, despite the gentle undulation of the craft as it bounced its way across the waves. She was carrying a tray with some tea and a selection of cakes. Having ordered the spread earlier, it had been prepared by the same steward who had assisted her with the luggage. Alice placed the mouth-watering array on an ornate low table alongside her mistress. "It's a very beautiful day and the hills look lovely," she said. "I could open the curtains for you, if you like."

"Don't be absurd, child!" Lady Olga snapped. "It's bad enough that I'm having to share this lounge with the other passengers. This ridiculous screen does not afford me nearly enough privacy, and I don't want it made even worse by being stared at through the glass by a gaggle of common people. I'm not in a goldfish bowl."

The irritable woman made no attempt to speak quietly. Her words carried beyond the screen and were heard by all those present. Conversations lulled and a hush fell.

"Ma'am, please," Alice implored, in a quiet though urgent tone, "the captain has given you a private section of the lounge all to yourself. That was the best he could do."

"Ha! The best, you say? When this journey is over I will be having words."

Then she looked down at the tray.

"I asked only for tea. Why have you brought cake as well?"

"I'm sorry, Ma'am, I thought you might like –"

"Why are you so incapable of following simple instructions? Take it away!"

"Yes, Ma'am."

As Alice leaned forward to pick up the tray, Lady Olga spoke again.

"Wait. On second thoughts, leave it. It will help me to pass the time while I'm incarcerated behind this miserable screen. You may pour the tea now."

Alice did as she was instructed, and then asked, "Will there be anything else, Ma'am?"

Lady Olga was about to speak, when instead she suddenly let out a shriek. It was loud and shrill, and caused the heads of numerous passengers beyond the screen to turn in her direction.

"What is that?" asked Lady Olga, holding out a trembling finger, and pointing.

Alice looked round and tried to sound re-assuring.

"Oh, that's just the ship's cat, Ma'am. I believe I heard one of the crew call him Dave."

"I can't take my tea with a … a mangy cat skulking around. The beastly thing is probably infested with fleas. Have it removed at once."

At that moment, Dave decided that this irate Russian woman was clearly in need of some calming comfort, so he sauntered across the lounge and began to rub himself affectionately against her shins, purring contentedly.

Lady Olga looked as though she were about to faint.

"Get this ghastly creature away from me" she yelled.

"Very good, Ma'am. I'll fetch one of the stewards to see to it. Will there be anything else?"

"If I need anything else I will call you! Just bring the steward and make sure this wretched feline is kept as far away from me as possible."

While the impatient Lady Olga waited for the steward to arrive, Dave the cat, who was blissfully unaware of the consternation he was causing, continued to foist his kindness upon her, weaving himself around her ankles, while she sat mortified and stiff as a rake.

Trying her best to stifle a smirk, Alice stepped away and disappeared behind the screen, re-entering the main area of the lounge. Here, there were a number of subdued passengers, the kindly colonel among them. All were standing silently, with some holding half-finished drinks. At the other end, the bartender stood behind a counter, giving too much attention to polishing the glasses, and deliberately not making eye contact with anyone, in an attempt to avoid the awkwardness which hung in the atmosphere like a lead weight.

"How do you put up with it, Miss?"

The voice at Alice's side startled her.

It was Denny Wright, the steward who had helped her with the luggage when she was boarding.

"Oh, it's you. You gave me a shock."

"Sorry, Miss. I didn't mean to."

"It's quite all right."

There was a moment's pause before he said, in a quiet voice, "I don't wish to sound impertinent, Miss, but could I have a quick chat with you in a few minutes?"

"Well … erm … yes, I suppose so."

"I have to go round and collect the empty glasses first, but after that I could meet you in the stern, on the lower deck? There's a spacious alcove beneath the staircase. Most passengers don't go there, so it'll be quieter."

Alice looked round at all the silent, long-faced passengers in the lounge, who were still feeling a little stung by Lady Olga's outburst.

"Could anywhere be quieter than here?" she asked.

Denny smiled. "See you in a few minutes, then," he said, and returned to his duties.

***

"We're not really supposed to talk much to the passengers, apart from pleasantries and taking drinks orders," Denny was saying, "but since, in our different ways, you and I are both servants I thought it would be OK."

Alice smiled but said nothing straight away, directing her gaze towards the beautiful scenery in the distance.

The two of them were standing, as arranged, hidden from view beneath the overhanging staircase, looking out over the lake as the cruiser made its scenic journey towards its first destination, which was Lakeside, with its quaint hotel and old fashioned railway station. Once there, many of the passengers would disembark before joining the characterful little train, drawn by a steam engine. Then, amidst great billows of steam – a testament to a bygone age – they would be transported the short distance to Haverthwaite, where they would be able to spend some time exploring the railway museum, before commencing their return journey.

Eventually, Alice decided that the silence had gone on for long enough.

"So, Mister…," She tilted her head and squinted at the steward's name badge, "Mister Denny, I'm all ears."

He smiled.

"It's not *Mr* Denny," he said, with a gentle chuckle. "Denny is my first name."

"Ah, I see. Very well then, Denny. What did you want to say to me?"

The young man gave a resigned shrug as he replied.

"To be honest, I thought I knew, but now that you're here I'm having trouble finding the words."

"Take your time," she said. "You have until we reach Lakeside to figure it out. After that, I'm afraid I will have to accompany Her Ladyship onto the Haverthwaite railway, where it won't be so easy to get away from all her moaning."

"Actually, that's what I wanted to talk to you about," said Denny. "You see –"

Just then, two figures, a man and a woman, appeared round the corner of the stairs. They stopped and gave the steward a hard stare. Denny suddenly appeared nervous and looked down.

"Is this fellow bothering you, Miss?" asked the man.

"What?" said Alice. "No, not at all. We were just having a friendly chat."

"A friendly chat?" This time it was the woman who spoke. "Is that all this is, Denny?"

Alice did not like the aggressive tone in the woman's voice, and an unusual surge of assurance rose from within her.

"May I ask who you both are?" she said.

The new arrivals each reached into a pocket and produced an ID badge.

"I'm detective Scott Jackson, and this is Diana Law."

"Law?" said Denny. "A fine name for a detective."

"Don't bother with the jokes," said detective Law. "I've heard them all before."

"So what actually is the problem?" Denny asked.

"Oh, there's no problem," said Scott. "At least, there won't be, so long as you behave yourself. We wanted you to be aware that we're keeping an eye on you – just for the time being. I'm sure you understand."

The two detectives began to walk away and climbed the stairs.

"See you around," Scott called, leaning over the bannister.

"Enjoy the voyage," added Diana, as they disappeared from view.

"I'm really sorry about that," said Denny, once the detectives had gone. However, unbeknown to him they were not quite out of earshot. Instead, they remained, hidden and out of sight at the top of the stairs, listening.

"What were they on about?" asked Alice. "They seemed so threatening."

"Trust me, you don't want to know."

"Try me?"

Denny paused, and exhaled, loudly. Then, quite suddenly, he seemed to fill with resolve.

"Sure, OK," he said. "Why not?"

He did not look straight at Alice, but instead gazed outward, over the waters and towards the rolling hills on the horizon.

"Basically," he began, "a few years ago I got mixed up with a bad crowd. I knew I shouldn't, but somehow I did. One thing led to another and … well … I ended up taking part in a robbery. At the time, I thought I was being really clever, but they caught me and I did some time inside."

Denny paused, and looked at the floor, feeling sheepish. Noticing that he was trembling, Alice reached out and put a hand on his arm.

"It's very brave of you to tell me," she said.

"Yeah, well, right now I'm out on parole, and those charming detectives you've just met have been sent to make sure I'm being a good little boy. If I put one foot out of line I'll be back inside as quick as you can blink."

"Denny," said Alice, "obviously, I don't know you at all. I mean … we've only just met, but you don't seem to be the sort of person who would get mixed up in something like that."

Denny smiled.

"Thanks for the vote of confidence," he said, "but it's true when they say that bad company corrupts good character. I did make some wrong choices, and I know that; but now I've paid for them and I just want to get my life sorted out and back on track."

"I'm glad to hear that," said Alice, "and when life inevitably throws any other obstacles in front of you, I have no doubt you'll be able to meet them with the same degree of resolve and determination."

"Thanks," said Denny, "I hope you're right. Actually, though, that's not what I wanted to talk to you about – the unexpected arrival of those detectives stopped me before I could get started."

Alice gave a little laugh.

"Oh, yes," she said. "I'd quite forgotten. Very well, then, what did you want to say to me?"

"Well, I have no wish to sound disrespectful, but the way your mistress has been treating you is really poor."

"Oh, she's always like that. It's just the way she is. I suppose she may have a lot on her mind at the moment."

"That's no reason to take it out on you – and to do it in public is unforgiveable."

"Please don't worry about me. I'm quite used to Lady Olga's tantrums."

"Still, behaving like that, sooner or later she'll get her comeuppance," said Denny, "and when it catches up with her it'll serve her right. In my opinion it can't come a moment too soon."

Alice then looked at the young steward, with what appeared to be an expression of genuine concern.

"You've been very kind," she said. "Bad things shouldn't happen to people like you."

"It's just life, I guess."

"Yes, but –"

At that moment, an ear-splitting scream was heard from somewhere inside the boat.

Alice and Denny glanced at each other, then rushed round the corner to see Lady Olga emerging from within. She was staggering along and leaning heavily on the balustrade. Her face had a grey pallor and the whites of her eyes were bloodshot. She did not look well, at all.

"Lady Olga!" Alice cried, and ran towards her, as other passengers moved aside, with looks of horror on their startled faces.

As Alice drew nearer, Lady Olga reached out towards her.

"Help … help … me…," she croaked.

Before the loyal maid could say or do anything, Lady Olga lost her grip on the railing and pitched forward into Alice's arms. By the time Alice had lowered her gently onto the deck, it seemed that she had stopped breathing.

"Doctor!" Alice screamed. "Is there a doctor on board?"

It was not certain whether her anxious voice had carried all the way to the bridge but, within moments, the captain was making an announcement over the tannoy.

"Attention please, this is the captain speaking. If we have a doctor on board today, would you please go at once to the starboard deck where we have a passenger who is in need of your immediate assistance. Thank you."

A group of worried fellow travellers had begun to gather round as Alice knelt with Lady Olga's head cradled in her lap. She was now no longer moving.

"Make way there, please. Let us through."

Detectives Jackson and Law shouldered their way through the throng and looked down at the stricken woman. Jackson crouched beside her and made a quick examination.

"I'm afraid she's gone, Miss," he said, looking at Alice, his expression impassive.

There was a sharp intake of breath from the onlookers as he spoke.

Just then, there was a slight commotion as one of the other passengers, a middle-aged man with a black bag, pushed his way onto the scene.

"I'm a doctor," he announced.

"I'm afraid you're too late, doctor," said Jackson, "but please still take a look at this woman. I'd like to see whether you agree with me about the cause of death."

As the doctor began his examination, Jackson stood up.

"Right, ladies and gentlemen, I must ask you to move away, please. There's nothing to see here, and the doctor needs room to work. Thanks for your cooperation." As he spoke, he and detective Law began to herd the people back along the deck.

After a couple of minutes, the doctor stood up and glanced at detective Jackson, who nodded and left his colleague, Diana Law, to keep the passengers in place. As he approached, the medical expert took him aside, and spoke in hushed tones.

"In all my years," he said, "I haven't actually seen a death like this before. Nevertheless, I do believe I have been able to establish the cause."

"Go on."

"It is most unusual, but, in my opinion, the deceased is showing all the signs of having been poisoned – with Melanicol."

Upon hearing this, the face of detective Jackson became grave.

The two men continued to speak for a few more moments – quietly, to ensure they were not overheard – after which the detective hastened to the bridge to speak to the captain. He then returned to the deck and made an announcement, by which point members of the crew had located a tarpaulin, and had used it to cover the now deceased Lady Olga.

"Ladies and gentlemen," said detective Jackson, "could I have your attention please?"

The passengers, looking anxious, turned to regard him.

"As I am sure you are all by now aware," he said, "I am sorry to have to confirm that we have had a fatality, and that it is necessary for my colleague and I to conduct a preliminary investigation before this boat can be allowed to dock."

"Conduct an investigation?" blustered the colonel. "What on earth do you mean? Are you suggesting there has been some foul play?"

"That is what we intend to find out," the detective replied. He then raised his voice as he continued. "Ladies and gentlemen, my colleague and I will need to ask you some questions individually. I have spoken to the captain and he has agreed that we can use the lounge for this purpose. Please be assured we will do our best to work as quickly as we can, to minimise any delay to your journey."

The assembled passengers muttered amongst themselves.

"And we may as well start with you." The detective looked directly at Denny Wright as he spoke. The young man rolled his eyes and sighed.

"I wonder why I'm not surprised," he said.

"Would you rather we did not ask you any questions?" asked detective Law, with a calculated degree of feigned surprise in her voice. "If you have nothing to hide, surely you would prefer to be eliminated from our enquiries as soon as possible."

At this, Alice spoke up, delivering her words with a confidence she did not usually feel.

"You're only starting with Denny because he's on parole," she said. "You've already decided he's guilty, haven't you?"

Her voice carried clearly, and the other passengers began to fidget and look agitated.

"Now then, Miss," said detective Jackson, "let's not raise our voices unnecessarily. We have formed no conclusions as yet. We just need to ask some questions to try and establish exactly what has happened here."

He then turned to Denny, and spoke again. His tone was civil and professional.

"If you would prefer," he said, "we would be quite happy to begin by questioning some individuals other than yourself, though please understand we would still have to get around to you, sooner or later."

Alice looked as though she was about to protest, but Denny spoke first.

"No," he said, "it's fine. Please, let's just get it over with."

"Thank you. In that case, please come this way. It won't

take long. Also, if you have no objection, I'd like to ask the doctor to join us too."

***

Despite all the apparent respectfulness which they had shown on deck, once the detectives had brought Denny into the lounge and were certain they were out of sight and sound of the passengers, they pushed him roughly into a chair and their tone quickly became markedly less polite.

"When you were talking to that young lady beneath the stairs," said Jackson, "you were overheard saying that Lady Olga would get her – now, what was the word?"

"Comeuppance," said detective Law.

"Comeuppance. Yes, that was it. You said she would get her comeuppance. Furthermore, you said that she deserved it and that it couldn't come a moment too soon. Would you care to explain what you meant by all of that?"

"Are you trying to suggest that I murdered her?"

"I didn't say anything about murder, Mr Wright."

"The young lady was distressed at the way she had been treated by her mistress in public. That bothered me, and I was simply trying to offer her some comfort and reassurance."

"Yes, of course you were. I'm sure that was the case."

There was a long pause, during which neither detective took their eyes from Denny, even for a second. The doctor, sitting quietly on a chair in the corner, was not enjoying this exchange in the least, and was trying to think of some reason by which he might legitimately excuse himself. Meanwhile, the young man was looking increasingly uncomfortable.

"Is something bothering you, Denny?" asked detective Law.

"No, no, I'm fine, really."

"I'm glad to hear that."

"So," Jackson continued, "let me lay this out for you, from our perspective, so you can hopefully understand the problem we have here. You came to the aid of this damsel in distress – a very noble thing to do. You clearly felt some sympathy for her and, perhaps in a moment of passion, announced that her mistress deserved some sort of punishment for treating her servant so badly. Then, just moments later, the poor Lady Olga drops dead. Now, that's an extraordinary coincidence, wouldn't you say?"

"If you are insinuating that I was in some way to blame for her death, perhaps you'd like to tell me how I could've had anything to do with it, since I was nowhere nearby at the time?"

"Oh, we've got ourselves a regular little Sherlock Holmes, haven't we?"

The sarcasm in Jackson's voice was unmistakable.

"The only way I could've bumped her off was if I'd poisoned her or something."

Both detectives now fixed the young steward with an icy glare.

"The cause of death," said Jackson, in a menacing tone, "was indeed poisoning. How could you have known?"

Denny blanched.

"What? I didn't know that. I was just saying. Anyway, I'd never met her before today."

"Irrelevant. This young servant girl suddenly found herself the object of your affections, and you couldn't bear the thought of her being mistreated. You've clearly never heard of a crime of passion."

"What? No! This is all nonsense!"

"We have discovered that it was you who took it upon yourself to prepare a tray of tea and cake for Lady Olga."

"What if I did? That's part of my job."

"This would have given you ample opportunity to add some poison to the unfortunate lady's tea, wouldn't you agree?"

Denny shrugged.

"I suppose it would have done, yes, but –"

"Ah, so you did poison her?"

"I didn't say that."

"Melanicol."

"What?"

"The name of the poison which was used to murder Lady Olga; it was Melanicol."

"Melani-what? I've never even heard of it."

"No, of course you haven't."

"Oh, for goodness sake, if I'd poisoned her I would hardly admit to the possibility would I?"

"Not unless you were being especially cunning," chipped in detective Law.

Denny threw up his hands in exasperation.

"What do I have to say to convince you people that I'm innocent?" he said.

"Would you be willing to submit to a search, sir?" asked Jackson.

"Oh, it's 'sir' now, is it?"

"Just trying to be polite, *sir*. I'll ask again. Would you be willing to allow yourself to be searched?"

"If that's what it takes to be rid of you, yes."

"Very well. Please stand up, place your feet apart and raise your arms above your head."

Denny did as he was instructed, and Jackson began a methodical search, patting him down and searching his pockets, watched by detective Law and the doctor.

"Look, I swear to you I'm innocent," said Denny, as the search continued. "I'm out of prison on parole and I just want to get my life back. I'm hardly likely to start going around murdering people am I?"

"In our line of work, we can never allow ourselves to jump to any such conclusion," said Law, before adding, as an afterthought, "sir."

Gradually and methodically, the contents of Denny's pockets were removed and placed on an adjacent table: his phone, keys, comb and wallet were all lined up in a neat row, along with a pencil and small notepad. They looked as though they were on some sort of identity parade.

"Aha … and what do we have here?" said Jackson, as he pushed his fingers into a shallow pocket in the front of the steward's waistcoat.

A puzzled frown crossed Denny's face at the sight of a very tiny clear plastic bag, containing what appeared to be a small quantity of some sort of light blue powder. The detective looked at it, curiously, and then looked at Denny.

"Would you care to tell us what this is?" he said.

The young man hesitated.

"Well, I … I don't know," he stammered.

"You don't know? OK, let's try something else. Where did you get it?"

"I … I don't know that either."

"Is it drugs, Denny, or something else? Something worse?"

The steward was sweating now, and he was looking decidedly ill at ease.

"I promise you, I don't know what that is, or how it got there."

"Take a seat," said Jackson.

Looking both worried and puzzled, Denny did so.

"Doctor," said the detective, "would you be kind enough to give us the benefit of your expert opinion?"

The doctor stood up and crossed the room to where the detective was holding the packet out to him.

"What do you think this is?" he asked.

The doctor carefully scrutinised the powder in the clear plastic packet, as he held it up to the light. Then he crossed to a table where he unfolded a serviette and carefully tipped a little of the powder onto it. He then picked up a teaspoon and ran its convex surface across the powder, to gain an idea of its texture. Finally, he went over to the sink behind the counter, returning a few moments later with a small cup of water. With a degree of caution, he allowed a single drop to land on the powder, after which he stood and watched. All the occupants of the lounge became aware of a faintly audible fizzing sound, before the powder lost its light blue colour and took on something of a pinkish hue instead, whereupon the doctor gave a quiet grunt of satisfaction.

"Well?" asked Jackson.

"Please understand that the tests I have just carried out are very basic. Until this substance is properly tested in a laboratory, it is not possible to give a sure confirmation as to what it actually is. However, –"

"Yes?"

"Initial indications suggest there is a strong possibility that this substance could indeed be Melanicol."

"Could you tell me, doctor, if this poison were to be administered, how much time would elapse before it took effect?"

"Again, it's difficult to say for certain, since it would depend on the size of the dose and, if any, the degree of natural resistance in the immune system."

"Understood, but can you make at least a rough estimation?"

The doctor thought for a moment.

"Please don't quote me on this," he said, "but I would suggest that once a person had been infected with Melanicol they would start to feel the effects about thirty minutes after ingesting it."

"Thank you, doctor, you have been most helpful. We will call you if we need you again."

The doctor nodded and left the lounge quickly, relieved to have been excused.

As detective Law leaned against the wall with arms folded and looking severe, Jackson began to move around the chair on which Denny was sitting. He walked slowly, while the steward looked at the floor and said nothing. Eventually, Jackson began to speak.

"Not looking good, is it, Denny?"

"I don't know what you mean."

"Oh, come along now, I think you do. Here you are, out on parole, with previous criminal history. You are overheard saying that a certain lady deserves what is coming to her and then, just a short time later she drops dead. As it happens, there is a doctor on board, though I suspect you hadn't anticipated that, who is able to identify that the cause of death is poisoning with Melanicol. Then – lo and behold – a routine search reveals that you are carrying some of the said poison in one of your pockets."

"I told you before, I don't know how it got there."

"Yes, I was listening."

"Anyway, there is no way I could have poisoned that woman. I've already told you I was never anywhere near her."

"True, but let's not forget that it was you who prepared her tea tray."

Denny's face became noticeably paler.

"Our good friend, the doctor, has just confirmed that the poison was, in all likelihood, administered around thirty minutes before death. I think you'll find that would tally quite neatly with when you were preparing the tray, wouldn't it?"

Denny remained sullen, and said nothing.

"Shielded behind the counter, it would have been the simplest thing in the world for you to add the deadly poison to the unfortunate Lady Olga's tea, completely unnoticed."

"I'm innocent," he said. "I didn't do it."

Detective Jackson drew himself up to his full height and spoke, clearly and boldly.

"Denny Wright, I am arresting you for the murder of Lady Olga Parchenko. You do not have to say anything, but anything you do say may be taken down and used in evidence against you."

As he was speaking, Denny failed to notice that detective Law had moved across the room and was now standing behind him. In a swift and sudden movement, she pulled his arms behind him and handcuffed his wrists.

"Let me go!" he yelled. "I didn't do it, I tell you. I didn't do it!"

"By now the captain will have radioed ahead, and a car will be waiting for you when we dock," said Jackson. "Don't worry," he added, "you will be given every chance to tell the truth, or otherwise."

***

In due course, the *Tern* docked at Lakeside, where two police cars and some stern-faced officers could be seen waiting on the dock. All passengers were requested to remain on board until the suspect had been removed.

While having to endure the ignominy of being frogmarched along an avenue formed of two rows of passengers and crew, the unfortunate steward was firmly propelled towards the gangplank by detectives Jackson and Law. The faces of those watching conveyed a variety of expressions: some displayed anger, while others looked sympathetic. The captain and first officer just looked sorry, but the colonel's face was indignant. As Denny was brought close to the top of the gangplank, there was the briefest moment of eye contact between him and Alice. He looked at her with a pleading expression but, although she tried her best to convey a feeling of being supportive, of course there was nothing she could do.

He was hurried down the gangplank before being bundled into one of the waiting cars and then driven away at speed. This unusual disembarkation process even caught the attention of Dave the cat, though after a few moments he lost interest and went wandering off elsewhere.

Thereafter, those passengers who wished to do so were allowed to disembark. Some began to make their way towards the nearby railway platform and the waiting steam engine, which had smoke already billowing from its funnel, to continue their journey to Haverthwaite. Others simply wanted to stretch their legs before re-boarding the boat for its return voyage up the lake.

Alice remained on board, going over and over in her mind the events of an extraordinary day. In one sense, it was a great shame that her mistress had met with such an unpleasant end. On the other hand, there was no question that her wealthy mistress was indeed a thankless, ungrateful woman. As a maid, Alice was very experienced. She did her job well, and had tried her very best to fulfil all of her employer's strict demands. Yet, in return, she had received nothing but a tirade of criticisms and derisory comments.

For all her guile and business acumen, the one thing the obnoxious Lady Olga had not learnt was that everyone has their breaking point.

Alice had reached hers some time ago.

Denny had been quite right when he said she 'had it coming'.

Although Alice had planned carefully, and knew that only one packet of poison would be needed, she had brought along a spare, in case of mishap. There was no way she could have anticipated such a stroke of good fortune, when a kindly steward, who was trying to help her with the luggage, would stumble against her and give her the perfect opportunity to slip the second packet into his waistcoat pocket.

Subsequently, as she was about to pick up the tray of tea and cakes which the steward had prepared, and while his back was turned, it was an easy matter for her to sprinkle the Melanicol into the teapot unseen and quickly replace the lid, before then carrying the tray to the waiting Lady Olga.

The final icing on the cake occurred while Dave, the ship's cat, was giving the vile woman such care and affection. While her mistress was screaming and shrieking and causing yet another scene, Alice spotted an opportunity and deftly snatched the woman's purse, popping it swiftly into the deep pocket of her skirt. Knowing that Lady Olga would have only thirty minutes from when she took her first sip of tea, Alice reasoned there was very little chance the absence of the purse would be noticed. Even if it were, there would be no time in which the battle-axe could do anything about it.

Then, a little later, she made her way to the meeting with Denny as arranged, discreetly dropping the now empty poison packet over the side as she went. No one noticed this action, except for the ship's cat, but Alice was confident that her secret was safe with him.

True, she was now unemployed. However, with all her experience and references she was quite confident that she would be able to find a new position quickly – good servants were in short supply and always highly sought after.

Looking over the railing of the boat, Alice became aware

that most of the passengers were now milling around on the dockside below, meaning she had the boat mostly to herself.

She walked to the counter in the lounge, where the crew member behind the bar snapped to attention and happily prepared for her the very expensive cocktail which she ordered. Reaching into her recently-acquired purse, Alice paid for the beverage with Lady Olga's money, adding a particularly generous tip and requesting that the drink be brought up to the main deck for her. Naturally, the steward was only too happy to oblige.

A few minutes later, Alice was seated on the deck in a very comfortable chair, sipping her drink and admiring the beautiful scenery.

It had been a perfect day.

Almost.

The one mildly irksome thing which still lingered in the back of her mind was regarding that friendly steward. What was his name again? Danny, or Donny ... or something. Alice couldn't quite remember, and it didn't matter anyway, but he had seemed like such a nice young man, despite his questionable past. It was a pity that he was going to take the blame for all of this, but no one ever promised that life was fair. Anyway, she knew that the awkwardness she felt at having such a memory would fade soon enough.

A few minutes later, the sound of the passengers re-boarding began to drift up from the gangplank below. Before long, the steamer would be on the move once again. At that point, Alice decided, she would order another of those deliciously pricey cocktails. While savouring every sip, she would relish the scenery and hear the soft, comforting sound of the waves gently breaking against the hull, as the *Tern* cut through the crystal clear, lovely blue waters, carrying her forward along the lake, and into whatever the future held.

Frank

No one paid old Frank any attention.

If anyone registered his presence at all, it was nothing more than a passing glance as they hurried past on the way to their departure gate.

If truth be told, the ancient cowboy had been sitting there for such a long time he had all but forgotten how long he had been waiting for his flight to be called, so that he and any fellow passengers could start boarding. However, since he had spent what seemed like half his life on trains, boats and planes, waiting in departure lounges had become second nature to him. While other passengers would huff and tut, and bemoan the length of time they had to wait, he was able, somehow, to put himself into a sort of 'stand-by mode'. Although he was, of course, still there in the midst of all the general noise and clatter, he was able to tune out, and distance himself from it.

So, right now, he had his eyes closed and his heavy, weary head lolled forward onto his chest. He was not asleep, as such; he just wasn't fully awake.

It was, perhaps, interesting to note that even though the

cowboy was waiting for his flight in Texas, a stereotypically Western area of America, he was the only person in sight whose attire actually made him look like the cowboy he was. While everyone else in the immediate vicinity was dressed in jeans, t-shirts, track suits and the like, he was every inch the traditional old timer. Leather rancher's boots, which were clearly handmade and expensive, complemented his tailored chinos. He wore a red gingham checked shirt, a bootlace tie and black waistcoat and, atop his aged head, a large, cream-coloured, ten-gallon hat sat resplendent.

The general hubbub of the concourse and waiting area was interrupted by a loudspeaker announcement.

"We would like to apologise again for the delay to your journey today, but we are now pleased to announce that Air India flight IN1265 to Mumbai will be boarding soon. Please have your boarding pass and passport ready for inspection. Thank you for flying Air India."

The final word of this public announcement seemed to permeate through to the dozing cowboy's consciousness and he was momentarily a fraction more awake.

"Indians?" he murmured, looking around. "Indians? Darn varmints! Where are they?"

But no one heard him, and a moment later his elderly head resumed its earlier position, slumping forward towards his gently rising and falling chest.

And, as he slumbered, the old timer dreamed.

In his dream, he was young again.

Young and agile....

He swung himself up into the saddle and spurred his magnificent horse to a full gallop. Racing towards the horizon, and silhouetted against the setting sun, he savoured the vast, open expanse of the prairie, and the wonderful feeling of the wind on his face....

"Sir? Excuse me, sir?"

"Hmm? What?"

Frank opened his eyes with a start, and it took him a moment to remember where he was.

"Are you booked on the flight to Mumbai?"

The young hostess looked down at him, with a professional smile.

"I sure am, Miss."

"Best to get on board now, sir. The plane is almost ready for take-off."

Looking round, Frank was surprised to find that he was now sitting alone in the departure lounge. Everyone else was already on the plane and waiting for him.

The elderly gentleman heaved himself to his feet, picked up his bag and shuffled towards the boarding gate, where he showed his pass, before making his way down the tunnel and onto the waiting aircraft.

As he stepped inside the plane, Frank allowed himself a slight smile when he glanced to the right, where the cheap seats were. Of course, in his younger days he had always travelled in the Economy section, as did all who were mindful of their finances. However, at this stage of his life, he could afford to indulge himself a little, so now he happily turned left and entered the heady surroundings of Business Class.

Notwithstanding the pleasure which this choice of upgrade provided, as the old cowboy was about to take his seat he did cast a furtive glance still further along the aircraft, where he caught a glimpse of the rarefied atmosphere in First Class.

Should he have pushed the boat out the whole way, he wondered, and really done this journey in style? No, he managed to persuade himself, he wasn't an aristocrat and he certainly didn't want to have to sit amongst people trying to convince him that they were. His Business Class seat would do him just fine. He was already looking forward to a comfortable snooze, once he was settled in and stretched out flat – a luxury denied to those travelling Economy.

A couple of minutes later, he had safely stowed all his luggage, and had neatly laid out his earplugs and blindfold on the tray-table. Then, just as he had eased himself into his seat a voice spoke at his shoulder.

"Would you like a glass of champagne, sir?"

He glanced up to see a young stewardess, who was immaculately attired and very pretty, holding a tray of the sparkling beverages which she was holding out to him.

"I see no reason why not," he said, with a smile. He took one of the tall, narrow glasses, not only noticing its bubbly contents, but also consciously registering the fact that the receptacle in his hand was indeed made of glass and not plastic. He had scarcely taken his first sip before an attractive selection of high quality nuts, olives and dates was placed before him too – and all without a single one of those awful, crinkly plastic packets anywhere to be seen. These had been tastefully arranged in a properly compartmentalised tray, and supplied with a linen napkin – *linen,* mark you, not paper.

Although, a short distance away, the sounds could faintly be heard of the common people down in Economy, somehow the décor and ambience of the Business cabin managed to create a feeling of serenity and calm. The cowboy leant back in his luxurious seat and gave a contented sigh. He sipped his champagne, ate a few of the nuts and, using the keypad in the arm of his seat, began to explore the selection of available movies on the screen in front of him. He did manage to find a couple of films which he thought looked appealing, though he knew that if he did decide to try and watch one of them, he would almost certainly fall asleep before the first twenty minutes had elapsed.

As he rode, the terrain became increasingly rocky and uneven. His horse slowed, first to a trot and then to a walk, as it cautiously picked its way across the undulating surface. Before long, high rock walls began to rise on each side as Frank realised he had ridden into a canyon. Casting his eyes upwards at the numerous outcrops of stone, fashioned by the elements over time into all manner of fantastic shapes, Frank felt an instinctive wariness begin to arise within. This would be a mighty fine place to stage an ambush, he thought to himself. I'd best get through and out the other end as fast as I can.

"Hello, sir. Would you like beef, chicken or vegetarian pasta?"

The question jolted Frank back to wakefulness.

"Hmm? Sorry? What did you say?"

"I apologise for disturbing you, sir," said the smartly dressed cabin steward.

"Oh, that's all right."

"We have a choice of meals for you today. Would you prefer beef, chicken or vegetarian pasta?"

"Oh, erm … I'll have the beef, thanks."

"Certainly, sir, and would you like something to drink with that? I have a nice Merlot which would complement the beef very well."

"I hate wine. Gimme a beer."

"Right away, sir."

He picked at the beef, but took little more than a couple of unenthusiastic mouthfuls. There was nothing wrong with it; actually, it was quite delicious, but Frank just didn't have any appetite right now. He'd always been like this on planes. In fact, over the years it had become so normal for him to end up handing back most of the meal uneaten he often wondered whether he should try asking for a reduced ticket price if he forewent the meal altogether.

He sighed and leant back in his seat again. He decided to attempt to watch a movie – an old black and white starring Gary Cooper. He knew he wouldn't stay awake to the end, but he had seen it before so that didn't bother him. The credits began to roll and the familiar music started playing, but even before the story got properly underway Frank's eyelids were already becoming heavy.

Before he had quite realised what he was doing, his years of experience, coupled with lightning fast instinctive reflexes, came into play; in the very nick of time he suddenly leant to one side as the feathered arrow sped past him, its sharpened tip of bone clattering against a nearby rock. He glanced in the direction from where the arrow had come but could see nothing. He had to get to some cover. Up ahead, in the shadow of the towering cliffs he could see some rocks that looked as though they might afford him some shelter. He began to head towards them, urging his horse to go faster, despite the uneven ground. The arrows kept coming and, as each one hurtled towards him, Frank could hear the whoosh as it cut through the air. They came from different directions, so he knew there were at least two Indians shooting at him. So far, all the arrows had gone wide, thankfully, but his horse had begun to sweat and was clearly nervous. Leaning forward, right up close to her neck, he patted her, and whispered. "Hush now. Stay calm, girl. Stay calm."

Narrowly avoiding yet another of the deadly arrows, he reached the cover of the rocks just in time and swiftly slid from the saddle. After leading his horse out of sight to relative safety, he crouched behind a large rocky outcrop. He drew his revolver and peered out at the steep, austere canyon walls, trying to gauge where his attackers might be concealed.

Without warning a large rock from the cliff face above plummeted to the ground and landed with a loud crash, only inches away from Frank's position. It shattered on impact, sending shards and splinters of stone flying in all directions. Then came another. Frank raised his arm to shield his eyes and face.

There was a sudden, aggressive bump, followed quickly by another, and Frank opened his eyes. Part of his mind was still occupied with his dream and, for a moment, he wasn't quite sure where he was. Then there was an electronic beep and an announcement was made: "Ladies and gentlemen, this is your captain speaking. You may have noticed that we have encountered some turbulence. I expect we shall be through it fairly soon, so there's nothing to worry about. However, I do ask that you return to your seat and fasten your safety belt. Thank you for your cooperation. Cabin crew, please discontinue the beverage service at this time."

Frank rolled his eyes. If there was one thing he hated about plane travel it was the turbulence, particularly when it was especially severe. This was not because it frightened him – it didn't – but because it disturbed his rest.

He glanced down at his in-flight entertainment screen. Gary Cooper was now involved in a shoot-out with some bad guys and his situation looked hopeless, but Frank, already knowing how the film would finish, paid it little attention. He glanced around at the other passengers in his vicinity, but no one returned his gaze; they were all attempting to read, sleep or watch a movie, all of which were rendered somewhat tricky as the aircraft continued to battle with the external conditions.

Frank reached out and picked up his blanket. After wrestling with it for a few moments, he finally managed to unfold it fully and then did his best to drape it over himself.

With the plane continuing to roll and bump as it was thrown around in the unstable atmosphere, Frank allowed his eyes to close and hoped that sleep would still be a possibility.

With revolver in hand, and while trying to remain alert to the possibility of further falling rocks, Frank leaned out from his position of concealment and risked glancing upward. As he did so, he was just in time to see the unmistakable tip of a feathered Sioux headdress protruding above the skyline before its wearer ducked back out of sight. He could not yet ascertain how many of these savages were attacking him, but from the arrows which had come in his direction he now knew there must be at least three, and possibly more. With great care, he positioned himself by a cleft in the rock, took aim at the spot where he had seen the Sioux warrior, and waited.

However, he did not have to wait long. There was a sudden flurry of movement, and the Indian's head was again in view. Frank's reflexes took over.

In the nearby galley, a member of the cabin crew had begun the process of stowing the meal carts. As he was doing so, the plane again flew into some sudden turbulence. The aircraft lurched, causing one of the restraining doors to slip from the steward's fingers and it slammed, loudly.

Frank squeezed the trigger and his weapon discharged its deadly missile. The sound of the shot echoed and bounced around the rocky canyon.

The sound of the slamming door was heard by one of the stewardesses, who came striding briskly along the aisle to assist her colleague.

Frank checked his gun and, with a shock, realised he needed to reload. He cursed under his breath and eased himself back into the rocky alcove.

The stewardess entered the galley to see the steward struggling to maintain his balance. With one hand he was trying to fasten the swinging restraining door, while the other was attempting to prevent a tray of cutlery from sliding off the worktop and onto the floor.

Assessing the situation in an instant, the stewardess darted forward, just as the cutlery tray slipped completely from the steward's grasp. As it fell, she managed to grab it, and was able to keep most of the knives and forks in place, but a few were dislodged and went clattering to the floor.

Just as Frank finished reloading, a volley of arrows came raining down. He was still sheltered by the rocks, so their finely honed tips bounced harmlessly off the hard terrain, but the sound startled his horse. She whinnied in fear and leapt to her feet. Frank called out to her but the poor beast was now terrified. Frank watched, helpless, as she fled the scene. Her flight, however, was slow, since she was hindered by the uneven surface.

Once his horse was some distance away, Frank was dismayed when he saw one of the Indians emerge from hiding and head towards her. He took aim but the warrior was too far away for any shot to be accurate at this range. He could only watch as the varmint took hold of her bridle, and his beloved steed was led away. A moment later, she disappeared as she was taken beyond the far rocks, and Frank felt his eyes start to glaze.

He was now alone.

In the galley, order had finally been restored, with virtually all items now stowed and doors securely latched. The fallen cutlery had been recovered and returned to its tray. It now sat on the level worktop, but it was decided that it would be best to relocate it to the plane's other galley, where a little more storage space was available.

Everything was still and silent – too silent. Frank, concealed among the rocks and holding his fully loaded gun, remained motionless and listening, trying to stay alert to any sounds which might occur – anything which might give an indication of where his attackers were, and what they might be up to.

Just then, he thought he heard something, though it was so quiet he couldn't be sure. Was it someone moving? The sound, if indeed there had been a sound, had seemed to come from over there … just behind those rocks. Slowly and carefully, Frank adjusted his position and took aim, waiting for the right moment to present itself.

As the steward was about to pick up the tray of cutlery, without warning the plane again struck turbulent air and heaved violently to one side. One of the female passengers screamed.

In an instant, an Indian brave suddenly leapt from hiding. Daubed with war paint and shrieking like a banshee, he took aim at Frank with his bow and arrows. However, with his gun aimed steadily,

Frank's finger was already curled around the trigger and he fired.

There was a sudden loud bang as the aircraft hit a particularly unstable patch of the atmosphere. In the nick of time, the steward managed to steady himself with a hand on the wall, preventing the knives and forks from tumbling to the floor a second time.

The warrior had a momentary look of surprise on his face as the force of the bullet opened up a gaping red hole in his chest and powered him backwards against the rocks, where he slowly slid to the ground, lifeless.

Now, all attempts by the band of warriors to move quietly were abandoned and it was immediately apparent that there were far more of them than Frank had at first realised. The braves gave forth ear-splitting war cries and screams, and Frank, shooting at as many of the Indians as he could, now found himself with arrows hurtling towards him from many different directions.

Finally, the plane levelled off. The sounds of turbulence vanished at last, and both the passengers and crew heaved a collective sigh of relief.

"This is your captain speaking. I hope you didn't find that experience to be too unsettling. Looking at the instruments here on the flight deck, I'm fairly sure we are now over the worst of it. However, just as a precaution, it would be sensible to keep your seatbelts fastened for the time being."

After dodging all the arrows and firing at the savages whenever he had the chance, Frank's gun gave out an ominous click. He needed to reload again. Cursing, he quickly reached for some more bullets.

But the pouch was empty.

His face paled as the grim truth hit home that he was out of ammunition. His gun was now useless and he was, to all intents and purposes, unarmed.

It did not take the band of Sioux warriors long to realise what had happened. Little by little — cautiously at first, but with increasing confidence and with wide, wicked smiles — they emerged from hiding and, with arrows aimed, drew near to the now defenceless cowboy.

The steward, holding the cutlery tray firmly, now began to make his way along the aisle.

The party of braves now encircled Frank. Their arrows were aimed; the string of their bows was taut and ready. Frank closed his eyes.

At the moment when the steward drew level with Frank's seat, the occupants of the plane were taken by surprise when yet another area of turbulent air was encountered suddenly, causing the aircraft to lurch alarmingly to one side.

There was a chorus of twangs as seven arrows left their bows and were propelled with force towards the lone cowboy.

The steward did his best to retain his balance, but in the process was unable to hold the tray level. A shower of knives and forks spilled out and cascaded onto the chest of the sleeping Frank.

"I'm terribly sorry, sir," blustered the steward. "Let me get rid of these for you."

He quickly removed the numerous items of cutlery from the old passenger's torso, being slightly surprised that the large man remained asleep while he did so. How could anyone sleep through that, he wondered, before then resuming his journey down the plane to store the cutlery safely at last.

***

The flight continued without further mishap and, in due course, finally landed at Mumbai airport. Even though the plane had touched down with a bit of a bump, the old cowboy slept right through it. Once the plane had come to a halt at the gate, there was the usual scramble as passengers pulled their luggage from the overhead racks and were eventually able to disembark.

Yet the cowboy remained asleep.

He was so peaceful and quiet that the cabin crew thought everyone had gone. It was only later, as they did a walk-through, that the slumbering man was discovered.

The steward placed a hand on his shoulder, and shook him, gently.

"Sir? Sir? Wake up, sir. We've arrived."

No response.

"Sir?" The shaking was a little more vigorous this time, and the tone of the steward became more urgent. "Sir?"

Then he saw the grey pallor of the face, and the blue tinge around the lips.

He turned, and called down the plane to the where the other crew members were waiting.

"Fetch the captain," he yelled. "Now!"

Greta

Her shoes were old. The leather was scuffed and faded, and the sole of each one was slowly but surely peeling away, as the once secure stitching which had held everything together was now becoming increasingly frayed and loose.

With the sun already sinking towards the far horizon, the young girl made her way through the chilly streets. The cold of the winter's afternoon, together with the sudden blasts of icy wind, bit into her as she plodded on with her head down and arms folded in a futile attempt to conserve some body heat. The thin fabric of her torn dress and the old shawl which was wrapped around her shoulders were no match for the low temperatures which assailed her, and it was all she could do to keep her teeth from chattering.

She longed to be back home.

If only she could be there right now, she thought – sitting there by the fire, gazing into its cheerful flames and feeling their emanating warmth coursing through her.

That was the way things had always been before.

But she knew she could not do that anymore.

At least, not at the moment – not while her Grandpa was

lying there, weak, hungry and alone, relying on her to bring him the food he needed to survive.

"You don't need to go out into the cold for me, dear Greta," he used to whisper, slowly, with an effort. "I don't want you to catch a chill. Anyway, the good Lord himself will take care of us and ensure we have all that we need, if we pray and commit ourselves to his tender care."

He had spoken with obvious sincerity and, while Greta would have much preferred to stay at home with her beloved Grandpa, she found that she was somehow not as able as he to rely solely upon the good Lord's mysterious provision.

If she and her dear Grandpa were going to have anything to eat, she realised, then it was up to her to go out and find it.

Although she had recently been quite ill, she had recovered, and her malady was now nothing more than a distant memory. This was most fortunate, because now it was her Grandpa who was not well, leaving her as the only one who could bring food into the house.

"Don't worry, Grandpa," she had replied, "I have no doubt that the good Lord will lead me to what we need and we will both soon be sharing a royal feast together."

This 10-year-old girl had a maturity beyond her years. She had spoken with outward confidence but inward despair, hoping that her quiet pessimism would not be noticed by her ageing ancestor.

As she spoke those words, her Grandpa had slowly turned his head towards her. His eyes, once full of light and life, nowadays seemed to be somehow less alive; and yet, as he gazed upon her, there seemed to surface from deep within a twinkling of admiration for the courageous little girl who sat beside his bed, holding his hand. Due to his failing eyesight, Greta couldn't be sure how clearly he saw her, or whether he even saw her at all. Sometimes, she found herself wondering whether he could even hear her when she spoke to him. Certainly, he himself did not speak now as much as he once did.

But he knew she was there – that was the main thing.

So now she trudged on, pulling her inadequate shawl closer, and endeavouring to ignore the cold in much the same way as the frequent passers-by ignored her.

As the shadows continued to lengthen and the temperature continued to fall, Greta encouraged herself with the knowledge that she had almost reached her destination. Sure enough, a few minutes later she rounded the corner, leaving behind the dimly lit side streets, and turned onto the main street of the small town.

Here, not only were the street lights bright, but further light poured forth from the many quaint shop windows. In addition, the numerous market stalls which lined the thoroughfare also had temporary lighting of their own – a variety of multi-coloured bulbs strung out on cables and wires – to illuminate their wares.

Greta ignored the shops; it was the market stalls that interested her. Although she knew each one of them would have been operating since the early morning, she always made a point of arriving towards the end of the day, when the prices of unsold stock would be reduced. Sometimes, if she happened to mention to a kindly trader that her Grandpa was sick, she could even obtain a few items completely free of charge, particularly if the stallholders knew they were unlikely to sell them at this late stage of the day. This was especially true of certain fruits and vegetables; where some were over ripe, or had become bruised, there was little chance that anyone would part with hard earned cash for such sorry-looking specimens. However, Greta was not put off by their appearance. She knew these cut-price items would still be just as nutritious and, anyway, once they were chopped up and added to a pot of homemade soup who would ever know what they had looked like on the market stall a short while before?

All of this meant that each time Greta embarked upon her quest for provisions she would do so without having any firm idea as to what she would actually bring home with her.

She made use of this fact in an attempt to cheer herself up, to create a feeling of anticipation and excitement, and to distract herself from the deep, penetrating cold which enveloped her.

Sometimes it worked.

Everyone else, she would say, has to make a shopping list; they have to plan which items they need, but not me. I can simply take whatever is available and save lots of time, trouble and planning in the process.

But her search for provender was not limited to fruit and vegetables. She was frequently able to obtain bread and rice too.

And, if she was really, really lucky, she would sometimes find that she was able to snap up a handy piece of meat or fish. Such offcuts, whilst not looking particularly attractive in themselves, would enhance nutrition and add an appetising, rustic flavour to a hearty broth – just the thing to keep the cold at bay on these lengthening winter evenings.

And, very, *very* occasionally, if she somehow happened to get the timing right, she even managed to pick up the final wedge from a wheel of Stilton, which was something she knew her Grandpa loved.

As time went on, it was increasingly the case that when Greta eventually returned home with her haul, it was already quite late, and she would find her Grandpa fast asleep.

If it was a day when she had been able to procure ingredients for a soup or casserole, she would quietly walk through to their small kitchen and begin to prepare a big potful which, she knew, would last for two or three days.

Alternatively, if on a given day she had only been able to bring home some fruit, she would place it, quietly, together with a knife, a plate and some water, on Grandpa's bedside table, so that it would be there waiting for him and he would see it when he awoke.

Then the little girl would curl up on her thin mattress over in the corner, and try to sleep, as best she could; or else, perhaps she might even venture out yet again, if she had reason to think that some additional location might yield further provisions, which were much needed.

***

After a lengthy though somewhat restless sleep, Grandpa opened his eyes.

He lay there for some time, not moving. Instead, he gazed up at the ceiling, noticing, not for the first time, how his imagination started to make pictures out of the cracks which covered it, like a network of veins.

And then he became aware, once again, of the quietness.

Absolute silence.

Nothing stirred.

He sighed and looked across at the selection of old black and white family photos atop the nearby chest of drawers. They reminded him of happier times in days gone by. As a single tear seeped from the corner of an eye it occurred to him how ironic it was that these events from long ago, recorded on glossy photographic paper, and which had brought him such happiness at the time, now caused him to feel sad and morose, as he resigned himself to the realisation that those days would not be repeated.

Half a smile played across his wrinkled face as his

memories caused these bittersweet feelings to well up from within.

A few moments later he was jolted from his reverie by a gentle knock on the door and the sound of the latch being lifted. The door was always unlocked – Grandpa was from a generation when friends and neighbours could call on each other at any time, without the need for an invitation, and without fear of anyone hostile seeking to gain entry or make mischief.

"Are you decent?" called the voice of the visitor.

"Never," Grandpa replied, with a chuckle, as he recognised the voice of his neighbour.

"Glad to hear it. In that case, I'm coming in."

Madge walked into the room. "I come bearing gifts," she said.

Grandpa looked up at her and smiled.

"You really didn't need to," he said.

"Of course I didn't," she replied. "That makes it all the more special, don't you think? These roses have come straight out of my garden, and I picked up these grapes for you from the greengrocer on the corner."

Without waiting to be asked, she plonked the grapes into a bowl on the bedside table.

"Don't worry," she said, as she saw Grandpa raise an eyebrow, "I asked the greengrocer to rinse them for me."

She then began to arrange the pink and yellow roses in a vase which stood alongside. After a few moments she stood back and admired her handiwork.

"There," she announced, "They really brighten up the room, don't you think?"

Grandpa smiled and nodded.

"They do indeed," he said. "Thank you."

"You're welcome. You'll need to remember to water them."

Madge then settled herself into the chair by the bed and the two of them began to chat about this and that. The various topics of conversation were somewhat meandering, and not especially interesting, but Grandpa was glad of the company.

After a while, and during a lull in the conversation, Madge glanced through the open doorway into the kitchen where she could see a pot of something had been left on the stove. She stood up and went to inspect it.

"I need to be on my way in a minute," she said, "But would you like me to heat up some of this stew for you before I go? It smells delicious."

"Stew? What stew? What are you talking about?"

"Oh, you are a funny old man sometimes. *This* stew – right here on the stove."

"But I didn't make any stew."

"Well it certainly wasn't made by me. Look, you're always doing this. How can you make such an appetising dish and then just forget about it? You must be having another senior moment."

"At the risk of stating the obvious, when you are a senior citizen, your whole life is made up of senior moments."

"Oh, you make me laugh. Honestly, you do. Wait there, you daft old thing, and I'll heat this up for you."

"Of course I'll wait. I'm not going anywhere."

***

If truth be told, whilst it did bother Grandpa that he could not remember making the stew, either on this or any other occasion, it was not the only thing which troubled his thoughts.

He had resolved that he would never mention this to Madge (since, privately, he disliked her repeated references to his senior moments) but sometimes he would wake up and find that some pieces of fruit had mysteriously appeared on his bedside table.

No matter how hard he tried, he couldn't account for how they had got there.

Not only that, but on other occasions it was bread and cheese that had somehow materialised; and not just *any* cheese, but Stilton – his favourite.

He knew that his mental faculties were not as sharp as they had once been, but he was pretty sure that if he had prepared these things himself he would remember having done so – at least on *some* of the occasions, surely?

The thin mattress over in the corner was empty, as always.

He hadn't been able to bring himself to remove it. Perhaps he would get around to it one day, he mused.

But it was just as well that it remained there, because this was the precise position where his granddaughter liked to sit and watch him – and that was exactly where she was right now.

She watched as he ate the stew she had made, and the cheese and fruit she had brought for him.

Each time, after he had eaten, there was something – though he couldn't quite place what it was – that caused him to look again at the row of grainy photos on top of the chest of drawers.

They were all of happy, smiling members of his family, with just one exception.

The photo at the end of the row had been taken in a cemetery. It showed a simple, plain cross, standing all by itself, separated from the other graves nearby.

"She was young, so young," he would sob to himself, over and over again.

Engraved into the stone surface of the cross was the single word, 'Greta.'

Frederick & Neville

The two friends made a point of meeting together once each week. By their own admission, at this stage of life neither of them really had much else to keep them occupied, so they really looked forward to their social afternoons; it did them both good to get out of their houses every so often, and spend a few hours reminiscing and laughing over a few drinks and a good meal.

They had only known each other for a little while, having first met shortly before retiring from work. However, a firm friendship had formed and they were each glad of this companionship in the autumn of their lives.

So, every Thursday afternoon, at 2.30pm, Frederick and Neville would arrive at their club. Although they did not particularly plan to reach the entrance at precisely the same moment, that always seemed to be exactly what happened. They would approach from opposite directions, see each other from a distance and wave. Then, after shaking hands, they would walk, side by side, up the steps to the imposing revolving door of the RAC Club on Pall Mall, where the immaculately uniformed doorman would smile and wave them in. They were now such regular attenders they were never asked to show their membership cards, though of course they always carried them.

They had selected the time of their meetings with care. Whilst they adored their club, with its air of sophistication and heritage, they also liked peace and quiet, so they would meet at 2.30pm, knowing that the high-flying, loud-voiced and over-confident businessmen who had been in for lunch would now be back in their offices and hard at work behind their desks.

This meant that Frederick and Neville, who were now both retired, had a good three hours of tranquillity stretching ahead of them before the dinner crowd arrived.

That being the case, they often found that the drawing room in which they sat to enjoy their pre-meal sherry was occupied by no one else. Then, when the Head Waiter quietly informed them that their meal was ready, they would walk through into the dining room, their feet treading softly on the deep pile carpet, and discover they had that room to themselves as well. Finally, they would adjourn to the smoking room to enjoy brandy and a cigar, again with seldom another soul to disturb them.

On those rare occasions when there did happen to be someone else present, it was always the case that they, too, were of the 'quiet' variety – just as Frederick and Neville were, and precisely the sort of person with whom they did not mind sharing the luxurious clubrooms. A smile and a polite nod would be exchanged with the other club members as they made their way to their chairs but, other than that, they would keep themselves to themselves, preserving the atmosphere of calm and conversing only with each other, in quiet tones.

Throughout the afternoon, at various intervals uniformed members of staff would silently appear, gliding through the rooms on missions unknown to Frederick and Neville, yet conveying the impression that all was well, that everything was at peace and under control.

Although the two friends had different tastes where their post-lunch brandy was concerned, they both had identical preferences for their pre-lunch aperitif. Their tradition of enjoying a schooner of Gonzalez Byass Amontillado had become such a regular part of their visit that the waiters, rather than asking to take an order, simply brought it to them as the two gentlemen took their seats in the opulent yet relaxed drawing room. There, relaxing in deep, comfortable chairs, they would savour the sweet, opaque liquid while perusing the lunch menu, which had also been provided without them needing to request it.

"That's one of the main reasons I like this place," Frederick would say. "The fact that the staff know what you want before you even ask for it is a sure sign of good customer service." Neville could only agree.

When it came to choosing what they would like to have for lunch the two friends had slightly different methods of arriving at their selection for that particular day.

"Are you going to break with tradition?" Frederick would ask, "Or are you going to stick with your usual method?"

"It's all good fodder here," would be Neville's usual comment. "I know that whatever I choose will be good, so, yes, I'm going to keep with my usual system." He would then add, with a grin, "If that's all right with you."

His 'usual system' was to work his way down the menu in order, from top to bottom, each week ordering the next item on the list, whatever it was.

Frederick's method bore a similarity to Neville's, but was still distinctly different; his procedure was to eat through the menu selections alphabetically.

Today, this meant that Neville's choices were rockfish

soup to start, followed by Bordelaise fillet of beef, while Frederick's alphabetical system directed him towards carrot velouté, with Cornish turbot to follow.

Naturally, the wine pairing was an intrinsically important part of the meal. By their own admission, however, this was something which neither of them was especially good at. Fortunately, the expert sommelier was on hand, as always, to suggest which fine choices would complement their selected courses and enhance the overall dining experience still further. On this occasion, after consultation with the wine waiter, they shared a carafe of New Zealand Sauvignon Blanc with their starters, while, for their main course, Neville took a large glass of Californian Shiraz with his succulent beef, and Frederick opted to have some chilled Chardonnay with his turbot.

They didn't always have desert. Sometimes, after the first two courses, they were just too full. Today, though, between them they chose a coconut and mango tart, and a guava cheesecake, which they shared.

As always, the meal was superb and, best of all, peaceful. The atmosphere within the club was so rarefied, it was almost impossible to think that just outside, beyond the walls of the building, there was all the hustle and bustle of a major city.

Later, once they had done full justice to their sumptuous repast, they adjourned to the smoking room, where they settled themselves into their usual positions in large, comfy armchairs before an open fire. On each side table, next to their chairs, a glass of Hennessey cognac had already been placed, along with two cigars, already cut and waiting to be lit; a Bolivar for Frederick, and a Montecristo for Neville.

This same ritual was followed, week after week, and the two friends enjoyed the conviviality enormously. What they especially looked forward to was the post-lunch conversation, where they would talk about all manner of different and, sometimes, unexpected things.

On this particular occasion, Frederick asked, suddenly, "How good are you with statistics and probabilities, that sort of thing?"

Neville's eyebrows rose.

"Statistics?" he asked, incredulous. "If you ask me, that sounds like a topic of conversation that's far too intellectual for our get-togethers; or too intellectual for me, at least."

"Oh, you're far too self-effacing," said Frederick. "The thing is, a thought occurred to me the other day. You know I was a music examiner for many years?"

"I did not. From time to time I have heard people say they have passed their grade two piano exam or grade five violin. Is that what you're talking about?"

Frederick nodded, and took another puff on his cigar.

"You already told me you were a musician," said Neville, "and you talked about recordings you'd made and performances you'd given, but this is the first time you have mentioned examining."

"In that case," said Frederick, looking surprised, "I apologise. Examining, in a way, used to occupy a large amount of my time and I was sure I'd mentioned it to you."

"Well, you hadn't, but now you have. So why do you bring it up, and what do you mean when you say it occupied your time 'in a way'?"

Frederick put down his cognac, carefully placed his smouldering cigar on the ornate ashtray and leant forward in his chair.

"Here's the thing," he said. "Every time I arrived to do an examining day, for each name on my list of candidates there would be five possible outcomes."

"I would've guessed two – pass or fail."

"Quite so, but there were also three others."

"There were?"

"Yes. If they did better than just a bare pass, they would pass with merit. Above that, the top candidates – those who had prepared really well – they would pass with distinction, which was the best result that could be achieved."

"All right, so that's four possible results. What was the fifth?"

"Ah," said Frederick, leaning back in his chair and taking up his cigar again. He drew a long puff before speaking once more. "The fifth possibility was that the candidate might be absent."

"Are you saying that someone would enter for an exam and then simply not appear?"

"Oh yes," Frederick replied with a snigger. "Absentees were always our favourites. They made the examiner's job so much easier, and it was far more common than you might think. In fact, that is the reason I brought up this subject with you in the first place. Sometimes the candidate might have been ill; sometimes the date they were given for their exam appointment may have clashed with something else, such as a family holiday or something. Another possible explanation is that they knew they simply hadn't prepared sufficiently. In that case, there was little point in turning up when they knew they were heading for a fail."

"But what does all this have to do with statistics?" asked Neville.

"Ha! Well, if anyone attempted to describe me as a mathematician," Frederick replied, "it would be a travesty. However, that label could be much more appropriately applied to you, wouldn't you say?"

Neville fidgeted in his chair and seemed a little bashful.

"Come along now," said Frederick. "Don't be shy. You're a genius with all things mathematical and were an expert in all the numerical jobs you did. Go on, admit it."

This was true. The fact was that over the many years of his working life, Neville had fulfilled a wide variety of roles, with each one requiring a secure and substantial ability in the realm of mathematical calculations. He had excelled in them all.

"Well," he conceded, "I suppose I did manage to garner a few commendations at various points along the way."

"Pah! A few commendations? You've got certificates and awards galore, not to mention that honorary doctorate from Cambridge."

Neville sighed.

"… and your point is?"

"Ah, yes. My point is this: I have a little puzzle which I cannot solve, but which I think might appeal to your numerically inspired brain."

"My dear fellow," said Neville, with a groan, "must you assail me with such a thing right now? We've just had a lovely lunch, we're relaxing with cigars and brandy and, to tell you the truth, I'm starting to feel slightly drowsy. I don't think my little mind could cope with any complicated mathematical problems right now."

"Oh, surely you can indulge me – just this once? There's another brandy in it for you."

Frederick gave one of his trademark winks as he offered his bribe.

Neville sighed and gave a wave of his hand.

"I am dismayed at being won over so easily," he said. "However, I must caution you that since I have yet to hear your question, I will not offer any guarantee that I can answer it."

"Understood," Frederick replied.

"Very well." Neville raised his glass as he spoke. "Proceed. I shall listen and fortify myself at the same time. After all, if another brandy is forthcoming I had better get this first one out of the way." He chuckled and took another sip.

"All right, then, here goes," said Frederick. He leaned forward in his chair, still holding his brandy, while the flames from the fire glinted and reflected in the fine crystal glass.

"Typically," he began, "each examining day would consist of around twenty-five candidates, with the vast majority of results tending to land in the pass bracket. Meanwhile, the smallest group was the absentees, with the fails, merits and distinctions coming somewhere in between. Not asleep yet?"

Neville shook his head. "Still with you, so far," he said.

"Good. Now, whilst there were never any hard and fast rules with this, you could be reasonably sure that at some point during the day, at least one of the candidates would be absent."

"That equates to a four per cent rate of absenteeism."

"Correct. I'm glad you're paying attention."

"I do try."

"Now, if the probability of there being one absent candidate in the day is one in twenty-five, what would be the chances of there being two no-shows?"

"Well, that would –"

"And, if we extend that thought still further, there must be a possibility, however slight, that there could be a day where no one appears at all. Would you agree?"

"In theory that would be possible, yes, though I have to say it is highly unlikely."

"Indeed, but now having established that a whole day of absentees would be possible, then my question becomes: what would be the chances of having two days completely free of candidates?"

"Well, it would take me a little while to calculate it, but I can tell you that as the number of absentees increases, the likelihood of two entirely empty days actually occurring would quickly become almost infinitesimal."

"Yes – though still possible?"

"Theoretically, yes, I suppose so, but I would have to say that it is really most improbable."

Frederick smiled.

"Let me tell you what happened to me," he said. "It was quite early in my examiner career. On one particular occasion, I was sent to conduct some exams in a parish church where a large number of the entries had been made by a school which was just next door. Well, it turned out that there had been some sort of miscommunication; somehow or other, the school had thought that the exams were still over a month away – and there was I, ready and waiting in the church to get started!"

"Oops! That was woolly-mindedness on someone's part," said Neville. "How long were these exams supposed to last?"

"I was scheduled to be there for a whole week!"

"My word! So what did you do?"

"Well, here and there, sprinkled throughout the schedule were a number of other candidates who were not from that school, so I still had to be in attendance to provide the exams for them when they arrived. Essentially, though, that week I had a very light workload indeed."

"Did you still get paid in full?"

"I did, thankfully, but that experience was when I first began to wonder about the probability of having whole days of no work."

"Ah, hence your question. Now I'm starting to understand."

"So, as I sat there, with very little to do in my official capacity, I began instead to use the time to work on my books – did I tell you I write fiction?"

"You did. Are they selling well?"

"Encouragingly so – thanks for asking. Have you got around to reading any of them yourself yet?"

"Ah, well…."

"Anyway, as that week progressed I learnt something about myself."

"Which was?"

"I realised that I really rather liked the notion of receiving full pay whilst doing very little work. Is that a bit naughty?"

"Ha! I'm sure there are many people who would subscribe to that view!"

"Well, as I pondered the statistical likelihood of such an easy week happening again, something else also began to cross my mind, causing the seeds of another, and altogether more crafty, idea to begin to take root."

"So I don't need to calculate those statistics after all?"

"No. I apologise. That was just my way of leading into this extraordinary tale."

"I'm relieved to hear that."

"However, there is still a link, as you shall see."

"You've certainly caught my attention, and I must say I am a lot happier now that I don't have to start trying to solve tricky problems after all. Do I still get my extra brandy though?"

"You see," said Frederick, ignoring his friend's question and speaking earnestly, "quite a number of years ago the exam board became aware that something rather deceitful was happening."

"Really? Whatever was it?"

"It had begun to emerge that some people would enter for an exam but, when the day came, would arrange for someone else to go along in their place, assuming their identity, to take the exam on their behalf."

"That's rather dishonest, isn't it?"

"Quite so. Shameful behaviour. Utterly, utterly dreadful."

As he spoke, Frederick was unable to keep a mischievous smile from playing across his lips. Even when he tried to hide it by taking another sip of brandy it was still quite obvious.

"Why do I get the impression that you are about to confess to something whilst feeling no remorse whatsoever?" Neville asked.

"Ha! Well, maybe I am, but we're both retired now, so what does it matter? Anyway, it looks like you need a refill."

Neville laughed. "Ah, now that you mention it…," he said.

Holding up his glass, Frederick signalled the waiter, who nodded and approached their table bearing the decanter with its precious liquid within.

A few moments later, the glass of each friend was refilled, the waiter respectfully withdrew, and the story continued.

"So," said Frederick, "there were two things that led me towards my selected course of action."

"Which were?" asked Neville, whose words were just starting to slur, a little. "You'll have to remind me."

"Firstly, the realisation that I wanted to be paid whilst keeping work to a minimum."

"You lazy so-and-so."

"Secondly, once it came to light that certain candidates were asking other people to take the exams on their behalf, I began to think that maybe two could play at that game. As I pondered, I wondered whether it would be feasible for an examiner to find someone to stand in for him!"

"Surely that must have been possible," said Neville. "After all, if an examiner were to be suddenly taken ill, a replacement would need to be found at short notice."

"That is correct, but I didn't want to have to wait until I was ill to take a day off."

Neville's brow furrowed.

"So what are you saying?" he asked.

"In a manner of speaking," Frederick continued, "I suppose you could say that I set up a sort of agency."

"I'm not sure I quite follow."

"You see," said Frederick, clearly warming to his subject, "not everyone who applied to become an examiner was accepted. In fact, the number of rejections was quite high. Not surprisingly, from time to time this resulted in some degree of hurt feelings, especially when the poor soul who was rejected was already a respected musician in their own right. I can tell you, Neville, artistic types don't like it when they are disregarded – it hurts their ego and pride."

"Do you include yourself in that?" Neville interjected, with a wicked grin.

"I will ignore that barbed question," said Frederick. "Do you want to hear how things went, or not?

"Oh, pardon me for even breathing," muttered Neville. "Pray, continue."

"Thank you. I will."

Frederick drew another lungful of the heady aroma from his Bolivar and sat back in his chair. This time, he did not return the cigar to the ashtray, but continued to hold it between his fingers, waving it gently in the air as he resumed his tale, sending slow, elegant twirls of smoke towards the tastefully gilded ceiling.

"Basically," he said, "this gaggle of disgruntled musicians, being certain that they could fulfil the role of examiner just as well as anyone else, effectively became my stand-ins. Every so often I would ask one of them to go and do a day of examining on my behalf, after which I would submit a claim for the fee. I would then deduct a commission before passing the remainder of the fee to them. I was successful in maintaining this façade throughout my time as an examiner.

It ensured that I had a liveable income, whilst not having to work very much, thereby releasing me to do what I really wanted, which was writing my books."

"But how could you get away with it, and for so long?"

"Actually, it was very simple. Naturally, as each candidate entered the room, they had no reason to suspect that the person sitting in the examiner's chair was not a genuine examiner. Equally, once the results arrived at HQ they had no way of knowing that they had been decided upon by someone else."

"A scheme as ingenious as it was cheeky," said Neville. "So, once this system of yours was underway, did you actually undertake any examining days yourself, ever again?"

"Oh, Neville, what do you take me for? Of course I did." Frederick leant back in his deep, comfortable chair and exhaled another plume of fragrant smoke, before adding, in a low and conspiratorial whisper, "But not many."

Cora

Cora's brow furrowed in bewilderment.

I must have been dreaming again, she thought to herself. Yes, that must have been it. There was no other possible explanation.

It was also the case that she hadn't been feeling very well lately, though even that was something of a mystery since her bouts of blurred vision, and moments where she experienced difficulty moving, were quite sporadic. She kept wondering whether she ought to go and see her doctor but then, just as she was about to make an appointment, the symptoms would disappear and everything seemed to return to normal once again. Cora was not the sort of girl who wanted to waste the doctor's time by booking a slot for no reason, so each time the symptoms vanished she would quietly hope that she had seen the last of them.

Her instinct, though, and subsequently her experience, told her differently.

Once again, she began to walk through the old house, passing through one room after another, all of which she knew so well. All were filled with such familiar items:

furniture, photographs, and ornaments galore. There were shelves piled high with books; tapestries and portraits adorned the walls, and the wooden floors and staircases gave a comforting creak as she passed over them.

Everything was in its proper place, just as it should be. All was well.

So why was her mind not letting her rest? What was disturbing her?

Though it was difficult for her to remember, the unusual occurrences had commenced, as far as she could estimate, several months earlier. How many of them had there been now? Cora couldn't remember with any real certainty, but she knew there had been quite a number of them, and it seemed to her that they were gradually increasing in frequency.

This was a source of genuine concern, since she was supposed to be taking care of her elderly mother who was lying in bed, very ill. Although her mother's actual room was upstairs, the staircases were becoming increasingly difficult for her to negotiate, so a makeshift bedroom had been set up for her on the ground floor. For much of the time, mother slept but, when she was awake, Cora would often come and sit on the side of the bed and they would talk.

Strangely, the conversation was always the same, even down to the exact selection of words.

"Have you found them yet?" mother would ask.

"Have I found what?" Cora would reply, though she knew the answer, since they had spoken about this many times before.

"The beads for my necklace," mother would answer. "I'm sure they're in the upstairs room at the far end of the house."

"No, I haven't found them yet," Cora would say. Although she had really tried to do so, her search for them had been hampered by other things.

"Do try harder, there's a dear," mother would say. "Once you have found them I can re-string them, and then my lovely necklace will be all back together in one piece again. It was the gift your father gave to me when he proposed. Did I ever tell you that?"

"Yes, mother, you did."

"Oh, he was such a fine gentleman."

The fact was that Cora had never laid eyes on this mysterious necklace. She assumed it must have met with some mishap when she was still very young, or possibly even before she was born. Now, all these years later, surely it was most unlikely that *any* of those missing beads could still be found, let alone all of them. It was much more likely that at some point in the past they had simply been brushed away as the house was being swept. Nevertheless, mother had repeatedly asked that they be found, and of course it would be so nice for her if her engagement necklace could be restored, so Cora always tried to be on the lookout for those elusive beads.

"But watch out for the bogeyman!" mother would warn. "He still thinks this is his house, and I'm pretty sure he and his helpers are still around here somewhere."

Cora would promise that she would be careful, and then she would quietly leave her mother's bedroom and softly close the door. Then, she would cross the large hallway and stand at the foot of the imposing staircase. Gazing upwards as the steps vanished into the darkness above, she would summon her nerve and begin her slow ascent, never sure of what she was going to find as she climbed towards the upper levels of this mysterious dwelling.

The problem was that the 'room at the far end of the house' to which mother referred was not particularly easy to reach. It was on the third floor, and it could only be approached by walking down a long passageway with numerous other rooms opening off it. Now, on the face of it, that shouldn't have posed any difficulty. However, each time Cora began to make her way along this dark thoroughfare her progress would always be disrupted by someone, or some*thing*, emerging from one of those side rooms, where sometimes the doors were open, and sometimes they were not.

Cora could never comprehend why her family had decided to move into such an eerie and unpleasant abode in the first place. Even more astounding was the fact that they elected to remain there, despite the plethora of unwelcome fellow residents on the third floor, some of whom were, in Cora's opinion, downright dangerous.

Once or twice, it did cross Cora's mind how strange it was that this assortment of unpleasant characters did seem to consign themselves to the upper floor, never venturing downstairs to where Cora and her mother were. That is to say, they had not done so up to now, so that was something to be grateful for, at least.

Cora's first frightening encounter had occurred the very first time she had attempted to negotiate the third floor corridor. Just as she was passing the first side room, whose door was standing slightly ajar, a long and excessively thick snake had come hissing and slithering its way out of the room and headed straight towards her. This evil-looking serpent had thick, leathery, red and black scales, which contrasted vividly with its glaring yellow eyes. Cora had been transfixed with fear, and found herself unable to move as the awful creature suddenly lunged with alarming speed, and darted towards her with fangs bared.

***

Cora couldn't remember running away from the snake – the experience had been so traumatic and severe that, by some means or other, she must have blocked it from her mind. Yet, thankfully, she had managed to escape somehow and, before she quite knew what was happening, had found herself back downstairs in mother's makeshift bedroom.

"Have you found them yet?" mother had asked.

"Have I found what?"

"The beads for my necklace."

"No, I haven't found them yet."

"Do try harder, there's a dear."

After this regular conversation had run its course yet again, Cora now found herself about to ascend the gloomy staircase once more.

This time, though, she came prepared.

She had remembered that there was an axe in the outhouse, where her father used to chop wood. Having run to fetch it, she now held it firmly in her hands and slowly began to climb the stairs. As she drew closer to the top, she paused and listened. That was when, above the sound of her own nervous breathing, she began to hear the chilling scraping of the snake's dry skin as it dragged itself across the uneven floorboards above.

Approaching the top stair, with her eyes now just above floor level, Cora could see the long passageway stretching ahead. At the far end was the room that was her destination and which, hopefully, contained her mother's beads. However, before she could reach it, she first had to get past the room containing the snake.

The door was still ajar, and she could hear the ugly serpent slithering within. If she tiptoed, as quietly as she could, maybe she could get past the room without being heard.

Little by little, and treading as lightly as possible, Cora

eased herself along. Having reached the top of the stairs, her heart was thudding inside her chest as she drew level with the door of the snake's room. Endeavouring to keep her anxious breathing quiet, she tightened her grip on the axe and continued to inch forward.

As Cora moved past the narrow opening, she could hear the sound of the snake's sinister movements even more clearly, and she hoped this meant that it was occupied with something other than watching her. As she crept along, and eventually began to leave the door behind, she allowed herself a silent sigh of relief.

Just then, there was a nerve-jangling squeal as her weight came to bear on a loose floorboard. Cora froze in apprehension. At the same moment, the sounds of movement from within the snake's room ceased. Was this heavy and chunky creature now aware of her presence? Cora stayed stock still, hardly daring to even breathe.

She didn't know how long she remained there, motionless, but the seconds felt like hours. Finally, she relaxed a little, and took another step along the corridor.

At that moment, there was a loud, angry hiss. Spinning round to face the door again, Cora was horrified to see the serpent launching from a coiled position and hurling itself through the air towards her. Instinctively, she side-stepped, while at the same moment swinging the axe in a deadly arc and, in a single blow, severed the foul creature's grotesque head from its body. With its eyes bulging, and its razor sharp fangs dripping with venom, the separated head rolled and bounced its way down the stairs, while the thick reptilian coils continued to twist and jerk as life eked away.

Still holding the axe, Cora became aware that she was trembling. Gradually, the twitching coils became almost still, now making only occasional sporadic jerks every so often. At last, Cora dropped the axe and leant against the wall, breathing deeply and staring at the remains of the huge, and now headless, serpent.

Once her racing pulse began to settle, Cora raised her head and looked towards the room at the end of the corridor. After an episode like this, she thought to herself, those blasted beads had better be there.

A few further steps along the passageway brought her level with the next side door. This one, too, stood slightly open. From within, a quiet buzzing sound was audible.

Cora did not want to investigate. What she *did* want was to go to the room at the end of the passage to find the beads for her mother.

And yet....

The sound of the buzzing had aroused her curiosity.

Cautiously, she took a step towards the door.

Just leave well alone, a voice in her head said.

That was wise advice, Cora knew, but she felt she just had to know what was causing that unusual noise.

She reached out her hand and gave the partially open door a push. The hinges squeaked and the door swung wide. The buzzing was louder now.

Although the room was dark, a little light from the corridor was able to permeate into the gloom. Cora took another step, peering up into the semi-darkness towards the source of the sound.

And then she gasped.

Close to the ceiling, in the furthest corner of the room, there was what appeared to be an enormous black ball, whose surface seemed to be moving.

It was a huge swarm of flies.

Larger than any flies which Cora had ever seen before, there must have been hundreds of them, if not thousands. Many of this seething mass of insects were constantly crawling over each other, while others hovered, seeking a way to take their place amongst the bristling conglomeration. Their wings were long and, as they flew, the buzzing they created was low pitched and menacing.

Suddenly, the sound seemed to become more focused, and much angrier, as a large number of the winged vermin swiftly detached themselves from the main swarm and, after circling around for a few moments, formed a dense pack and headed straight towards Cora with alarming rapidity.

Cora screamed. She turned to run from the room, and tried to slam the door behind her, but many of the hideous winged creatures were able to get through before she did so. They crowded in upon her, flying round and round, buzzing madly, landing on her and crawling into her eyes, ears, nose and mouth. Cora shrieked and staggered around, waving her arms in a desperate and futile attempt to defend herself against this frenzied onslaught.

***

Yet again, Cora had somehow managed to escape. As always, though, she had no recollection of how she had done it, and now, once more, she found herself back in her mother's room on the ground floor.

"Have you found them yet?" mother asked.

"Have I found what?"

"The beads for my necklace."

"No, I haven't found them yet."

"Do try harder, there's a dear."

Cora left her mother's room and went first to the outhouse, from where she had fetched the axe last time, returning a few minutes later. This time she had equipped herself with a large canister of fly killer, to which she had attached a length of garden hose.

She again began to climb the stairs. Upon reaching the

upper landing she averted her gaze as she passed the severed snake's head, whose eyes still glared, and whose fangs still protruded. Then, in the corridor above, passing the room from which the snake had emerged, she carefully picked her way over the serpent's motionless headless coils, before nearing the second open door.

As she approached, the now familiar low pitched buzzing became audible once again. Cora gulped but tried to hold her nerve as she took up a crouched position by the door. Then she slowly reached up and, grasping the handle, began to pull the door closed. The squealing hinges cut through the sound of the buzzing and seemed to catch the attention of the winged creatures. For a moment, the buzzing quietened, but then it regained its ferocity with renewed vigour. From what she could hear outside in the passage, Cora could tell that hundreds of members of the swarm had separated themselves from each other and were now heading rapidly towards the door. This time she managed to slam it shut just as the first insects arrived on the other side; she could hear them flinging themselves against the wooden surface, their angry buzzing becoming louder with each attack. Cora quickly pushed the end of the hosepipe through the narrow crack under the door and opened the valve on the canister. There was an encouraging hiss as the insect poison was propelled along the pipe and into the room beyond.

The flies were immediately aware of this invisible attack upon them and renewed their assault on the closed door. However, their efforts were futile. Within moments, the sound of buzzing began to falter and quieten. From her position out in the corridor, Cora could hear their large, fat bodies as they dropped to the floor, where they continued to try and use their failing wings to become airborne once again, but it was no use. The poison did its job with great efficiency, and the room was soon silent.

Once Cora was certain there was no further threat from within, she heaved a sigh of relief and closed the valve on the canister. Now there was no longer the hissing of gas, nor any buzzing of wings; the passage was eerily silent.

Exhausted, she lifted her head and looked down the corridor. Seeing the door at the far end gave her a feeling of renewed energy. Standing to her feet, she began to move towards it.

Along the way, Cora passed a number of other doors, all of which were closed. She was happy to let them stay that way, and relieved that nothing emerged from any of them.

However, as she finally reached the door that was the goal of her mission, and just as she was reaching out to take hold of the handle, she heard the sound of a click from one of the doors further back along the passageway, followed by the unmistakable sound of hinges squeaking.

Her heart skipped a beat. What ordeal was she going to have to face now?

She looked round to see a slightly rotund, middle aged man emerge from one of the rooms. He looked ordinary and normal enough, causing Cora to relax slightly, but who was he? And what was he doing in their house?

The man saw her and nodded.

"Good afternoon," he said.

Cora was about to reply, but before she could do so, the man had turned his back, and began to make his way along the corridor away from her. Cora wasn't sure what to do now. Ought she to follow him? After all, what business did a stranger have, being on an upper floor in a house not his own? On the other hand, she had been trying to get into this end room for some time, and now she finally had her opportunity.

Before she could make up her mind, the man stopped

walking. He was looking at something which was lying in the passageway.

"That's my axe!" he exclaimed. "How did it get here?"

He turned round and fixed Cora with a piercing glare.

"How did it get here?" he repeated, more loudly this time.

"Well, I ... erm...."

"Have you been using it? Have you been using my axe?"

"A snake attacked me," Cora whimpered.

The man had picked up the axe now, and had begun to walk purposefully towards her.

"You," he hissed, between gritted teeth. "You used my axe – without asking permission!"

"I'm very sorry."

"How dare you! How *dare* you!"

He came nearer.

And nearer.

"Stay away! Stay away from me!" Cora shrieked as she began to wrestle with the door of the end room.

As she pushed and pulled at the unyielding door, suddenly she became aware that a shadow had fallen across her.

Terrified, she looked round.

The man stood over her, holding the axe above his head. His expression was one of intense anger.

"Do you know what they call me?" he asked. Then, more loudly, "Do you?"

Trembling, Cora did not speak, but shook her head.

"They call me the bogeyman. Do you know how much I hate that?"

Cora tried to push herself back against the door, in a subconscious attempt to get as far away from the man as possible, but it was no use; the closed door ensured she remained where she was.

"And not only that," the man continued, "but to make it

worse, they have the sheer audacity to take and use my things without my permission!"

"I'm sorry ... sir," Cora whimpered. "I didn't realise the axe was yours, truly I didn't."

The man's voice now rose to a shout.

"And, as if that were not bad enough," he yelled, "after they've used my things they don't even have the courtesy to put them back where they found them."

Cora looked up into the thunderous, glaring face, and began to weep.

"Well, I've had enough of it," the man bellowed. "Enough! I've tried to be patient, but now you need to learn your lesson. Do you have any last words, little girl?"

He tightened his grip on the axe handle and raised it even higher.

Cora wanted to run. If she was quick, perhaps she could dodge around this lunatic and escape, but suddenly she found that she was incapable of moving at all.

The axe blade glinted as it paused in mid-air, waiting for the moment to begin its deadly descent.

Cora almost screamed, yet even her scream would not leave her throat.

She felt completely paralysed.

Yet the man appeared to be faltering and hesitating too.

Although the axe looked as though it were about to come plunging down, it remained motionless, held aloft in the air by the mad axe-man, whose face bore an expression which was frenzied, yet unmoving.

Time itself seemed to come to a standstill.

***

"Aww, no! No!"

Billy's father looked up from his newspaper.

"What's the problem?" he asked.

"The computer's crashed again."

"Again? Sorry about that, son. There must be a bug in the programme or something."

On the flickering screen, the image of a young girl cowering while an axe-wielding maniac stood over her was held, motionless.

"It always does this, at exactly the same point," Billy moaned.

"Have you tried re-starting the game?"

"Of course."

"What about re-booting the whole system?"

"Tried that too. It's so frustrating, 'cos each time I have to start the level from the beginning again. I really want to open that door and see what's inside the room at the end, but every time the axe-man appears this is what happens."

"Have any of your friends had the same problem with theirs?"

Billy nodded.

"Actually, yeah, they have. It looks like this same problem has cropped up in a whole batch of these games."

"Okay," said his dad. "At the weekend we'll take it back to the shop and get a replacement or a refund."

"Thanks. In the meantime, I suppose I may as well have one more try. I guess it might work this time – you never know with computers."

Dad shrugged.

"Ain't that the truth," he said, and resumed reading his newspaper.

Billy selected the option to replay the level and focused on the screen.

"Have you found them yet?" mother asked.

"Have I found what?"

"The beads for my necklace."

"No, I haven't found them yet."
"Do try harder, there's a dear."

David

David had always been a quiet, reserved child, who kept himself to himself.

True, he did have friends, but he did not often spend much time with them. He preferred his own company and his solitary pastimes, such as reading and model making.

At school, he was very able, being blessed with a particularly strong imagination, which helped him to write stories on all kinds of subjects, and with a level of detail which was very unusual in one so young. During free-choice periods, while other children would be running around shouting, and playing games, David was much more likely to be found in the book corner of his classroom, either engrossed in the pages of a fantasy tale, or else jotting down story ideas of his own for future use.

Although his parents were quietly concerned at their son's apparent disdain for social interaction, they were sure he would grow out of it in due time; his academic prowess and creative ability more than made up for any shortcomings elsewhere.

It was when his pets started dying that the problems

began.

One morning, he had been awoken by the sound of an urgent knocking on his bedroom door, and the voice of his mother telling him to get up straight away.

Still rubbing his tired eyes, David had come staggering down the stairs and had walked into the living room where his parents were waiting. Both of their faces bore expressions of sadness and sympathy, as they moved aside and allowed him to see what they had discovered a couple of minutes earlier.

At first, everyone assumed that David's guinea pig and his two mice had met their untimely ends thanks to the claws of the family cat. However, his fur and whiskers were devoid of any tell-tale signs which might have suggested that he was the guilty party, and he was strutting around and meowing in a manner that was, seemingly, an attempt to proclaim his innocence. Gazing down at the bloodied and mangled balls of fur, David cried silent tears.

If the cat *was* to blame, David was angry with him.

But he loved him too.

Someone must have left the cage door open by mistake, his father suggested.

But David would not have made a mistake like that. He was always so careful. After feeding his beloved animals, he always made sure the cage was latched securely.

He did.

Always.

And he'd done it this time too.

Hadn't he?

Yet no one else ever went near the cage, so there seemed to be no other plausible explanation. He reluctantly agreed that, in a rare moment of not thinking, he must have left the cage door open, which enabled the cat to seize his opportunity.

His parents tried their best to engage their son in activities which, they hoped, might take his mind off the tragedy, and it almost worked. A few days later, though, when the cat was found dead too, it was more than little David could bear.

David had put his cat's food and fresh water into their respective bowls, as he always did, and then rattled the open window to signal that the meal was ready, as he also always did, but when the cat did not appear from his afternoon ramble, which was very unusual at dinner time, David went out to search for him.

He didn't have to look very far.

He found his much loved cat in the alley, close to the back gate.

Its head had been smashed in.

He couldn't believe it. David's emotions were a mixture of shock, sadness, despair and rage. Who would do such a thing? It must have been one of the boys from 'over the way' who went to that other school. Who else could it have been? They were always idly hanging around on street corners or getting up to mischief. Yes, it must have been one of them, he decided.

However, there was no proof of this heinous act and, with the mystery unsolved, and now being left without his furry friends, from whom he had derived so much comfort and companionship, David became increasingly insular and withdrawn.

What little interest he had had in playing games with his friends was lost, and his schoolwork began to suffer. Eventually, the head teacher asked his parents to come into school for an 'informal chat' to see if they could figure out what could be done to help restore David to his previously happy and contented self.

A plan was formulated and, a few days later, a delightfully playful puppy, whose name was Sparky, took up residence in David's house. The little boy and the little dog took to each other immediately and it certainly seemed as though steps were being taken towards healing the wounds from the recent past.

But, not long after, the visits began.

***

The bedtime routine was always the same.

Each evening at the appointed time David would dutifully climb the stairs to his room, change into his pyjamas and get into bed, where he was allowed to read for a little while before lights out.

Then, he would reach down and give a loud knock on the floor. This would inform his mother, who was downstairs in the sitting room, that he was ready to sleep.

Sometimes she would come up straight away. Sometimes there would be a short pause while she finished talking to David's father about something or other; or sometimes, the wait would be because she wanted to finish some sewing or knitting, or else see the end of a television programme.

If she didn't come right away, David would sometimes give a second knock, in case mother hadn't heard the first one. Of course, she *had* heard it – she always did – so, occasionally, this second knock would result in her calling up the stairs with a slightly irritated tone, "In a minute!"

Then, satisfied that she had heard after all, he would lie back on his pillow and wait patiently. He knew she had heard, so he knew she would come.

Mother always came.

And, when she did, this was the one thing about bedtime that he really loved.

For those few, beautiful moments, it was as though nothing else in the world existed.

Mother would sit on the sheepskin rug next to his bed and lean both elbows on the blankets. Then with her head turned to a slight angle she would wink at her son and give that delightful smile which David loved so much.

And then they would talk.

They would talk about whatever things may have happened during the day – whether it was something at school, or in the park, or something that had happened to one of the neighbours – and they might talk about whatever was planned for tomorrow. Sometimes, even though David had, technically, already had his full quota of reading time, his mother would offer to read him an extra story.

This was what David always hoped for.

He loved it when his mother read to him, so when the opportunity presented itself he always tried to choose a longer story, rather than a shorter one, as he knew this would extend the time that she would stay with him.

She would read with expression and enthusiasm, and David found himself easily whisked away into far-off lands of legend and myth, where powerful beasts and wicked witches did battle with knights in armour and other dashing heroes.

He loved these times with his mother, not only because they were so special in themselves, but also because they delayed the thing about bedtime that he hated.

Inevitably, the moment of parting would come.

Mother would do that thing (which David also loved) where she would put one of her arms each side of him, push down firmly on the blankets and say, "Snug as a bug in a rug!" Then she would lean forward and give him a kiss on the forehead.

As she was about to leave the room, she would pause by the door and look back at her son, lying cocooned beneath several layers of blankets, providing protection against the cold night air.

Then she would smile again, before saying, "Night night, sleep tight, see you in the morning light."

And then she would leave, closing the door softly behind her.

And then David was left, alone.

Alone in the dark.

And then began what he hated about bedtime.

In the darkness of the room – and whether his eyes were open or closed seemed to make no difference – he saw all manner of different coloured shapes which would float in and out of his field of vision. When they stayed as amorphous shapes it wasn't too bad, but sometimes they would shift and change into the heads of monsters and demonic creatures, which would parade past him, in a never-ending line of foul vileness.

David didn't like it but, to be fair, this endless procession of fiends never looked at him or acknowledged that he was even there.

What *did* bother him, however, was the other thing.

It wasn't always there, but it was there more often than not.

The *presence*.

David kept trying to tell himself that it was all just in his imagination – that it wasn't real – he was just making it up.

And yet it *was* there. He knew. Right there, in his room, standing at the foot of the bed.

David couldn't see it, because of the darkness, but he knew it was there, and he knew what it looked like.

It was a large, muscular man with a huge, bushy beard, who was staring straight at the place where David was lying. He was bald, and had a thick neck. Beneath his vest he was covered in evil-looking tattoos, and he was holding an ugly-looking knobbly wooden club. Some nights, when the visitor came and stood there, David's terrified heartbeat seemed to be amplified, so much so that it would fill the room. When this happened, the giant would give a mirthless grin and begin to knock his club against the end of the bed. Somehow he always knew exactly how to synchronise the speed of his knocking with David's frightened pulse.

David knew that because of the darkness this silent watcher couldn't actually see him, yet the giant knew he was there, and if David so much as moved – or if he even breathed – his position would be revealed and the giant would attack.

Now, the closeness and security he had felt when his mother was with him felt a million miles away. Even though he was sometimes faintly aware of her voice as she chatted away downstairs, the *presence* in the room all but obscured it, and David knew he had to endure the intrusion of this uninvited visitor alone.

Sometimes, he wished that he were stronger. He wished he was no longer a child. If he was a grown-up he wouldn't be afraid. Grown-ups weren't afraid of anything. He would spring out of bed, snatch up his baseball bat and defeat this evil giant with a single blow – just like one of the heroes in the stories his mother would read to him.

Only … he wasn't a grown-up; he was just an eight year-old little boy.

So he would lie there, motionless and afraid, for a very long time.

He knew that, no matter what, he must not move.

And yet, somehow, he also knew that if he moved very, *very* slowly, and very, *very* quietly, he could assume a more comfortable position in his bed without the giant being aware of it.

And then he would be safe.

So, slowly – ever so slowly – he would roll over onto his

side, and quietly – ever so quietly – he would take hold of his favourite teddy bear and hold him closely to his chest.

Then, if his eyes were not already closed, he would close them, satisfied that he had somehow managed to evade detection by this visiting terror of the night.

Then he would whisper to his teddy – ever so softly, just in case the giant was still listening – "Night night. Sleep tight. See you in in the morning light."

And the next thing he knew, he was opening his eyes. It was morning, and during the night the giant had, at some point, slipped away.

***

But all that was a very long time ago.

Thirty years ago, to be precise.

Even now, during the long, dark hours of the night he would sometimes dream about the pets from his childhood; he still missed them, very much, and the brutal way in which they had departed this life still caused him to shed an occasional tear.

And the sudden disappearance of Sparky, who had vanished without a trace, still haunted him. Even now, he had no idea as to what had become of him.

That was why he had no pets now.

Sure, he would've liked to have some – or at least one.

Another puppy, or a kitten perhaps.

He loved animals.

But, given his history, where he seemed to be incapable of guaranteeing his animals' welfare, he felt sure that any unfortunate creature that came into his possession was bound to be going on a very short journey with a one-way ticket to – well, wherever animals went once they threw off this mortal coil.

In his mind, and when he was alone, he could still hear the sound, all those years ago, of that insistent knocking on his bedroom door, when the bad news was revealed to him by his parents.

But that was three decades ago. Things had to move on.

David was now a successful company manager, overseeing the operations of the local branch of a major travel agent, with responsibility for the motivation and performance of a contingent of twenty-five staff.

He was still single – a fact which irked both him and his parents – but he was hoping that would change soon; you see, there was this girl in his department whose job, amongst other things, was to deal with any complaints which came in by phone – and she was drop dead gorgeous.

Sally had the most alluring deep brown eyes; she had a smile like David had never seen; and she had an infectious giggle which was guaranteed to put a smile on the face of all but the very hardest of hard-nosed people. Somehow, whenever she answered the phone, no matter how aggressive the tone of the caller, and no matter how justified the complaint might be, she had that special knack of being able to calm the situation and work out a resolution to the problem that kept all parties – and the rule book – happy.

In a role like that, she was worth her weight in gold.

David knew it and, secretly, he loved her.

Some time ago, he had decided to ask her to go on a date.

It was a risk, but he would do it.

He really would.

Just as soon as he could summon the courage.

After all, she was a sophisticated young lady, with real finesse, and she simply might not be interested in someone like him.

And he couldn't bear the thought of being rebuffed, so the operation would need to be planned very carefully.

***

One evening, after a particularly long and tough day, during which an unusually large number of ticket bookings had been made (which was good) and an unusually large number of complaints had been received (which was not so good) David arrived back at his apartment very late, exhausted.

He couldn't face preparing a meal at this hour. So, instead, after dumping his jacket over the back of a chair, he poured himself a generous glass of his preferred beverage – vodka and orange, with perhaps a little too much vodka – kicked off his shoes, settled himself into his favourite reclining chair, grabbed the remote and switched on the TV.

In truth, and despite some diligent channel surfing, there wasn't really anything on the screen that interested him at the moment – the programmes he really enjoyed came on much later – so he settled for one of the news stations and sipped his drink, watching for a while, though without really taking anything in.

But then, something the newsreader said caused him to suddenly sit up.

That can't be right, he thought. I must've mis-heard.

He swiped up the remote once again and increased the volume, as the newsreader continued.

"… and police have now confirmed that the person was unlawfully killed. The victim was found dumped in a rubbish container this evening by refuse workers doing their nightly collection in the alley that runs parallel to the high street, behind the *World Tickets* travel agency…."

World Tickets was where David worked, and his mouth fell open in disbelief.

But that wasn't the worst of it.

"… formal identification has yet to take place, but an

examination of the deceased resulted in the discovery of credit cards and a driver's licence which give the name of the victim as Sally Jenkins…."

WHAAT??

David couldn't believe it. There must be some mistake. There is no way this could have happened – not right behind his workplace. Not to Sally. He had been talking to her just a couple of hours ago, for goodness sake!

"… according to the local coroner, the cause of death appears to have been a heavy blow to the head with a blunt instrument. Police are trying to contact relatives, but any family members are asked to call this number…."

***

Naturally, David couldn't get Sally out of his mind, and he cursed himself for not having had the nerve to ask her out. If he had, maybe she wouldn't have been alone this evening. Maybe she would've been with him. Maybe things would've turned out very differently.

But now, the time had passed.

The opportunity had been lost.

David dabbed at his moist eyes with a tissue, unable to decide whether he was more sorry for Sally and the way she had met her grizzly end, or for himself – for the loss of all that might have been. Was he destined to live his entire life on his own?

He needed another drink, and was about to pour himself another glass of vodka, when he decided, instead, to simply take a large swig straight from the bottle. He stood, quietly, savouring the moment as the smooth, chilled liquid glided down his throat. Then he went and placed the half-full bottle on his bedside table. He would need it later tonight, he decided.

After such an awful day, he deserved it.

Later, when he finally climbed into bed, he was so preoccupied with his thoughts of Sally, that he was caught somewhat off guard when the nocturnal visitor from years before quietly returned.

It had been such a long time since he had felt that … that *presence* at the end of his bed, that he had all but forgotten about it.

But there was no mistaking it. One moment, it hadn't been there; but then, a moment later, it most certainly was, and the tendril of fear that David had felt as a child ran down his spine once again, as the doors to his memory were flung open, and the images of the past returned.

However, the difference between then and now was that David was no longer a child. Holding the edge of the duvet up to his chin, he peered out into the darkness and spoke to the unseen guest, trying to project a boldness that he did not entirely feel.

"If you had to come back, why did it have to be today? Don't you know I've just had some really bad news?"

The visitor said nothing, but David knew he was staring straight at him, and hefting the wooden club in his large, strong hands.

He was about to speak again, but then he heard something.

That sound.

The knocking.

The giant was knocking the club against the end of his bed.

David found his voice again and spoke into the darkness.

"Why do you do that? And how did you know where I lived? How did you find me?"

He wasn't really expecting a reply, since the giant had never spoken to him during any of his previous visits.

But this time, the knocking stopped and the visitor spoke.
The voice was gruff and deep.
Menacing.
"I didn't have to find you. I never left."
The knocking resumed.
Slow, and measured.
"What do you mean, you never left? I haven't seen you for years."
"Of course you haven't, but I've always been here."
"Would you please stop that knocking?"
The knocking continued, and David could feel the sense of apprehension and foreboding from his childhood years trying to rise within him once again.
But he could also feel something else: a realisation and, with it, a growing indignation.
Because, quite suddenly, everything fell into place, and he knew.
He knew, but he almost wished he didn't.
He tried to make his slightly trembling voice sound stable and assertive as he spoke again, slowly and almost firmly.
"Did you … did you kill my pets?"
No answer.
Only the continuance of that infernal knocking.
"You did do it, didn't you? Answer me!"
At last, the knocking ceased, but there was still no verbal response.
As his anger grew within, so did David's confidence.
"How could you do that?" His voice was rising now. "I was only a child. How could you take my mice away from me, and my pet guinea pig?"
Still no answer from the apparition at the foot of the bed.
Distraught, David reached out for the bottle of vodka on the bedside table and took a large gulp.
"And my cat – I loved him." He began to sob. "I loved

him dearly, and you took him from me. Why? Why?"

"I did not do it."

The knocking began again.

"Stop knocking!"

The knocking continued, louder now, and a little faster – a little more urgent.

"And my puppy! My Sparky!" David now had to almost shout to make himself heard above the noise. "We all thought he had just wandered away and got lost – but you killed him as well, didn't you! My poor Sparky. How could you do that? How could you take a child's pets away from him? What sort of monster are you? Have you no conscience at all?"

"I did not do it."

And still the knocking continued, and David realised it was now accurately keeping pace with his heartbeat, just as it used to do.

"Oh, really? You didn't do it? OK then, Sherlock. *If* you didn't do it, are you going to tell me who did?"

No answer.

In the darkness of the room, David sensed that the visitor had begun to slowly back away. He knew that he was leaving.

"Wait! Where are you going? Stop! You can't go now. I forbid it! I want some answers."

Then David became aware that as the giant retreated into the shadows, the knocking of the club on the end of his bed had somehow transformed and had now been replaced by another knocking sound coming from somewhere else in his apartment. This transference from one to the other was unmistakable, yet seamless.

"What now?" he yelled. "Can't a man sleep peacefully, even in his own home?"

He threw back the duvet and stood up.

The knocking was even louder now.

Cursing under his breath, David cast a longing glance at the bottle of vodka on the small table, then left his bedroom and half walked and half staggered his way along the corridor.

The knocking was coming from his front door.

He glanced at the clock.

Bloody hell! It was 2.30am!

He reached the door but didn't open it.

"Who's there? Do you have any idea what time it is?" he shouted.

At the sound of his voice, the knocking ceased.

"Sir, we are sorry to disturb you. This is the police. We just need a quick word. Could you open the door please?"

The police? What were they doing here?

He opened the door to see to three uniformed officers and another man who had the appearance of being some sort of plain clothes detective.

David rubbed his eyes.

"What's all this about?" he asked. "How can I help you?"

"Are you David Curtis?"

With a quizzical look on his face, David nodded.

"David Curtis who works at *World Tickets*?"

"Yes. Couldn't this wait until the morning? What's going on?"

"Are you aware that a few hours ago one of your employees, Sally Jenkins, was murdered?"

"Yes, I heard about it on the news. Dreadful business. She was such a lovely girl."

"We heard from her friends that you became rather angry with her when she turned down your offer of a date."

"What? No ... no, that was nothing – just a simple misunderstanding."

"David Curtis, I am arresting you for the murder of Sally

Jenkins. You do not have to say anything, but anything you do say may be taken down and used against you in a court of law. Do you understand?"

Before he could respond, two of the uniformed constables had stepped forward and each grasped one of his arms.

"No!" David cried. "You've got the wrong man. It wasn't me! I didn't do it, but I know who did."

"Really, sir? And who might that be?"

"It was the giant. He did it! It was him. I know, because he was just here and I was talking to him. He carries a heavy club. That's his weapon. He even killed my pets."

The detective rolled his eyes, but nodded to the other constable who quickly stepped inside and walked round the apartment, returning a few moments later. He looked at the detective and shook his head.

"The giant doesn't seem to be here anymore, sir. Let's just take a nice easy trip down to the station, shall we? We'll be able to get everything sorted out once we arrive."

"But it wasn't me," David whimpered. "I could never do anything like that."

"Of course you couldn't, sir. Please come along with us — there's a good fellow."

***

A few minutes later found the bewildered David sitting secured in a steel mesh cage in the back of a police van.

"Why is this happening?" he whispered to himself.

Why hadn't the police believed him when he'd told them about the giant? Surely it was obvious that he was the one they should have been looking for.

Suddenly the van went too quickly over a speed hump, causing David to be thrown upwards a couple of inches before landing again with a jolt on the hard seat.

More so than the preceding events of the evening, he found that the abruptness and severity of this bump unsettled and unnerved him. In the darkness of the police van, he became aware, once again, of his racing heartbeat. Why did it always seem so loud?

Looking down at the floor of the van, he took some slow deep breaths, and tried to calm himself.

But then he realised that what he was hearing was not just his heartbeat alone. There was something more.

A knocking.

A knocking that David had heard before.

The knocking.

With a start, he glanced up.

A few feet away, at the other end of the cage, sat the tattooed giant.

He was still holding the now familiar wooden club, and was knocking it softly against the floor of the van, in time with David's heartbeat.

David had been under the impression that he was the only occupant of this cage in the van. However, now that he saw this familiar figure he felt a surge of confidence.

"Ha! So they did catch you after all. Now you're in for it! I hope you get everything that's coming to you. You deserve it."

The giant spoke – but only once; the same words he had used before.

"I didn't do it."

"Well, you would say that, wouldn't you? Let's see if you change your tune once we reach the police station."

With a self-satisfied smile, David turned away and looked out through the darkened glass to the outside world. There was nothing to be seen through the tinted window, except for the sudden flash of streetlights as the van passed by.

"And would you *please* stop that knocking!"

As he spoke, he swung round to face the giant again.

The tattooed man was nowhere to be seen.

In the darkness of the cage, David was alone.

But the knocking continued.

And it swelled.

Louder and louder.

Louder and louder, until it drowned out the sound of the van's engine.

Louder and louder, until it obscured the sound of David's anguished screams, as he began to roll on the floor of the cage with his arms wrapped around his head, in a futile attempt to shut out the din.

Louder and louder, until it exceeded the angry shouting of the police officer in the front, ordering him to be quiet.

"Please ... please stop the knocking...."

David was sobbing now, as he begged for the unrelenting racket to cease.

Yet it continued.

"Please...."

And *still* it continued, even louder than before.

Always the knocking, always....

"Please stop ... please...."

Edith

***

Dear Reader,

The tale that follows is deliberately very short, and here is the reason why:

I was once challenged to see whether I could write a complete story using exactly one hundred words (not including the title) and this is what I came up with.

Due to the limitation on the number of words, descriptive detail is, of necessity, in short supply here. However, I have every confidence that the fertile imagination of my loyal readers will be more than sufficient to fill in any blanks.

Enjoy!
R.S.

***

As she placed the expensive bottle of champagne atop the rest of her high quality groceries, Edith smiled.

Not for her the bargain range and cheap instant noodles.

Then, her smile faded. Glancing around, to be sure no one was watching, she left the trolley, piled high with its array of tasty delights, and walked out.

She crossed the road and entered a tiny corner shop, emerging a couple of minutes later with a carrier bag containing a small, sliced loaf and a tin of baked beans.

With head bent into the cold wind, she began the walk home, alone.

Gerald

Each morning was the same.

The middle-aged multi-millionaire would leave his suite of rooms, which was booked permanently in his name at the Dorchester Hotel, and make his way down to the dining room, where he would take his usual seat at a table which had been set for four persons.

Naturally, he could have made alternative arrangements and had the breakfast brought up to his room; it would have been more expensive, but money was no object for him. However, the arrangement that had been made was to meet in the dining room, so that was the plan he stuck to.

A sumptuous array of items was available at the breakfast buffet, covering a cosmopolitan selection; there were varieties to cater for all tastes. For a start, there was the full English breakfast: eggs, bacon, sausages, baked beans, tomatoes, hash browns, mushrooms and black pudding, supplemented with cut fruit, freshly baked bread and pastries. However, for those who were looking for something a little more exotic, there was a Lebanese section, containing a huge array of olives, and oil infused roasted vegetables. There was an Indian counter, displaying lamb and vegetable curries, as well as roti canai. For the health conscious, there was a well-stocked salad bar, plus steamed rice and chicken, as well as Asian delights such as nasi lemak and nasi goreng, with all the associated condiments. There was even a Japanese corner, displaying a mouth-watering variety of beautifully presented handmade sushi of many different colours and kinds.

There was a time when all these delicacies would have attracted him, but no longer.

His tastes were much simpler now.

Each morning he would help himself to an ordinary bowl of cereal, with some semi-skimmed milk. After that, he would fetch two slices of wholemeal toast, with some raspberry preserve and a pot of Darjeeling tea.

He wouldn't need anything else.

If he was honest, he didn't really seem to have much of an appetite these days.

However, although his choice of breakfast items was small compared to the large selection available, these were not the only things he brought to the table.

For each of the other three place settings, he obtained a glass of fresh orange juice and positioned each one just so. There were other options, of course, including mango, grapefruit and water melon, but he knew that orange was their favourite.

He was confident that when his family arrived they would certainly want to take full advantage of the large selection of items on offer. Many times, he had been tempted to pile up a plate of food for each of them, so that it was there waiting for them when they arrived, but he always decided against doing that, since he didn't want it to go cold.

But there was no such problem with the orange juice, of course.

So, there he would sit, and each day he would have his cereal, tea and toast, and then stay there, until long after he had finished, regarding the three untouched glasses of orange juice, waiting.

Just waiting.

Waiting for his family.

And he went through this same routine every morning.

***

Two years earlier…

It was a consistent source of irritation to him that he simply could not remember when or how everything had started to go wrong.

He had always given his family the best of everything.

At least, that is what he had tried to do.

Had he really failed, so miserably?

At first, everything had been fine.

Or, at least, it had seemed so.

Gerald's only worry had been the possibility that when he 'popped the question' his beloved might say no. Thankfully, she hadn't, and he and his bride-to-be had enjoyed a fairy-tale whirlwind romance, which swiftly culminated with an exchange of vows at the altar of their picturesque village church, on a perfect, sunny day.

Not long afterwards, a baby had arrived, with yet another soon after that.

Both parents were delighted. All four of them bonded well together and they became a stable family unit.

As well as being, stable, Gerald had thought they were happy too.

He really did.

They wanted for nothing.

Income was healthy, and in no danger of running out.

The house was lovely.

The kids were great.

They had the world at their feet.

So why, and how, had everything gone so wrong?

One day, he had returned home to find a note that had been left on the kitchen table. It was written in the petite, distinctive and instantly recognisable handwriting of his wife. Since then he had read it and re-read it so many times that he could now remember it by heart, word for word.

Dear Gerald,

Please don't ask me why I am doing this – I'm not sure I fully understand it myself.

Recently, I have felt like there has been a growing distance between us. We don't seem to connect and communicate like we used to, and I don't know why or how this has happened.

All I do know is that I need to get away, and I need to take the kids with me.

I need time to think.

Please don't be angry. Maybe we'll be able to get back together sometime.

Regards,

Judith.

The fact that she had walked out on him, without any warning, was bad enough. However, what really stung him was that penultimate word in her message – *Regards*.

What?? *Regards*? What about … 'with love' … or, at least, 'best wishes'?

Regards….

Of course, he did try to call her, but it appeared that she had changed her number, as all of his numerous attempts to contact her were answered by a very unsympathetic electronic voice which told him that the number was unobtainable.

For many days afterwards, he wandered in a state of mental unrest, unable to think or concentrate on his work or, for that matter, on anything else. The bottom had dropped out of his world and he felt utterly bereft.

Although those early days of separation were dark indeed, of course as time went by he gradually grew accustomed to his new situation, and managed to regain a little focus on his work, and life in general, but he never fully recovered from the shock – not really.

Whilst he had always paid lip service to the notion that money could not buy happiness, he now learnt that painful truth at first hand, and with full force. Despite the many millions which he had stashed away in various accounts, and despite his numerous attempts to lose himself in expensive pastimes, the simultaneous paradox of his absent family and the all-consuming emptiness which accompanied it, were never far from his mind.

No matter what he tried to do, and no matter how he tried to fill the void, one loud, unanswered question continually screamed at him from the depths of his soul.

Why?

Why?

All he had left was the note that Judith had written. He had lost count of the number of times he had almost thrown it away; but, for some reason, he found that he could not bear to part with it. Since it was the last thing he had received from her, albeit bringing bad tidings, he wanted to hold on to it.

Furthermore, the note itself was the only thing he had that threw any light at all on her decision to leave, though the information it contained was scant, to say the least. There was the note, and that was it. There was nothing else

– no further explanation had been offered, and there had been no further contact from her at any time since. There had been no mention of divorce and, perhaps surprisingly, neither was there any demand from her for any form of financial support.

She had, quite simply, gone.

Vanished.

She had taken the children, who were the delight of his life, and left.

The nagging question, therefore, remained.

Why?

***

Then, months later, something extraordinary occurred.

After many long days and nights of soul searching, Gerald had finally managed to begin to exercise some degree of control over the emotional upheaval which the disappearance of his family had caused. During the intervening months, since the moment of separation, he had wandered aimlessly, in a sort of daze, going through the motions of doing his work to try and stay occupied, but with no real sense of focus or purpose.

But then, just as things were at last starting to regain some semblance of balance, and as he was managing, after a fashion, to adjust to his new 'normal'....

A second note arrived.

He didn't see it straight away.

He scooped up the several items that had been pushed under the door of his hotel suite and carried them wearily through to the kitchenette, where he dropped them onto the table while he prepared a cafetière of his favourite Colombian coffee.

Once the brew was ready he carried it across to the table

and sat down.

He picked up the first envelope and sighed.

Some sort of junk mail, which he just couldn't face reading.

He placed it to one side and took a sip of the coffee, savouring its rich aroma and taste. After placing the hot beverage back on the table, he picked up the next item.

A bank statement. Ho hum. And then an advert from the hotel, announcing special prices on their massaging service.

He was already reaching for his coffee once again; but then, as he looked towards the next envelope, which had now reached the top of the small pile of communications, his heart skipped a beat.

He would have recognised that handwriting anywhere.

The coffee was forgotten as he grabbed the envelope, tore it open and removed what was inside.

Just a single sheet of notepaper, folded in half.

With trembling fingers he unfolded it and began to read.

Dear Gerald,

I hope you are well.

The children are fine and always ask after you.

I was wondering whether it would be possible for us to meet up for a chat soon. My plan is to come to your hotel at 1pm on Wednesday and it would be lovely to see you, if you're free. Of course, I realise you may not be available. If that's the case, don't worry — I'll wait for 20 minutes or so and then be on my way.

Hope to see you soon,

Judith.

He read and re-read the note many times. The piece of paper bore no address, and there was no mention of a phone number.

But at least she had contacted him — that was the main

thing.

Wednesday!

The day after tomorrow.

Well, of course he would be free. He would make certain of it.

He called his secretary and ensured that all appointments were re-scheduled.

And then he waited.

And he had never known an intervening twenty-four hours to last so long.

***

The day came.

When Gerald awoke that morning he was a mixture of excitement and nervousness unlike anything he had known before.

He had set his alarm for 7.00am, but had actually been wide awake since well before 5.00am so, when it did start to ring, it startled him.

Having washed, shaved, dressed, and then checked his appearance in the mirror more than a dozen times, he made himself a cup of coffee, but decided he wasn't going to bother with any breakfast, since he was certain that the butterflies in his stomach would prevent him from keeping any food down.

He glanced at the clock.

7.30am.

Still only 7.30?

The 1pm meeting seemed to be an eternity away.

Why were the hands of the clock moving so slowly? Gerald stared at them, trying, by sheer force of willpower, to make them increase their speed. When that didn't work, he picked up the morning newspaper and skimmed through the various headlines, but found he couldn't concentrate on any of them. So he turned, instead, to the hotel TV, and tried to focus on the news bulletins and weather reports, but the numerous voices on the screen seemed to blur together into an incoherent babble, and he was unable to take any of them in. Finally, he resorted to the newspaper's cryptic crossword – something he would never normally even look at, let alone try to actually complete it.

Not surprisingly, he was unable to determine a single answer to any of the enigmatic clues.

The layout of his suite of rooms was such that is was possible to walk a circular route through them, and this he now did, from the kitchenette, into the dining room, then into the bedroom and finally reaching the living room, before then being able to re-enter the kitchenette again. He paced round and round, a countless number of times, pausing only to glance at the clock and occasionally to look out of the large picture window, which commanded an impressive, panoramic view of Hyde Park and the city, spread out far below.

More than once, in a somewhat futile attempt to break the monotony, he turned round and recommenced his circular walk in the opposite direction.

The time dragged, and continued to do so.

Though the minutes felt like hours, and despite the fact that the hands of the clock seemed to be stoically immobile, it was nevertheless the case that they *were* actually moving and, little by little, the time of the meeting drew steadily closer.

When 12.30pm was eventually reached, Gerald could not contain himself any longer. He left his suite, and walked the short distance along the carpeted corridor to the elevator, where he then descended to the ground floor and stepped out into the hotel lobby.

The meeting with Judith was set for 1pm, of course, but he wanted to be there early to avoid any possibility of missing her.

For some reason, the lobby seemed to be busier than normal. Usually, by this time all the hotel guests who were going to check out would have left, while those who were due to check in would not yet have arrived, creating a lull in the general level of activity. Today, however, it was crawling with people. Every available seat was taken, either with people or luggage, and the reception staff appeared to be run off their feet, with lengthy queues at each desk.

Then, glancing through the revolving doors, Gerald glimpsed a large luxury coach parked outside and realised that most of the people in the lobby were from some sort of sports team. Many of them were wearing uniformly designed navy blue tracksuits, and there was a countless number of sports bags and pieces of equipment, piled high on hotel trolleys, with the gang of hotel bellboys doing their best to stack everything safely, before beginning to wheel the many pieces away to their respective intended rooms. Amongst the team members there was much loud chatter, with frequent use of expletives, prompting guffaws and further ribaldry.

Gerald sighed.

Of all days, today was the one when he wanted the hotel to be quiet and peaceful.

Even so, there was still almost half an hour to go before Judith was due to arrive, so hopefully everything would have quietened down by then.

The final minutes ticked slowly by.

Sometimes, Gerald would look at his watch. At other times he would watch the clock that hung on the wall behind the reception staff. When not keeping an eye on the time, he was watching the revolving doors. There was a fairly constant stream of people going in and out, and, amidst all the hustle and bustle, he didn't want to miss her.

Then a thought struck him.

Would she be bringing the children along too?

She hadn't mentioned anything about that in the message and, in the circumstances, it seemed a little unlikely; but, then again, she hadn't said she *wouldn't* be bringing them, so at least there was a chance. Gerald felt his sprits lift still further as he contemplated seeing his wonderful offspring, and all of them being together as a family again, even if it was for only a short while.

He looked up at the clock again.

Not long now.

***

The moment came, and the chiming of a clock on the roof of a nearby building informed anyone who was listening that it was now 1 o'clock.

Much to Gerald's frustration, the level of busyness in the entrance hall of the hotel had not abated. Amongst the buzzing hive of activity in the foyer, a vacant seat *had* now become available, but Gerald was not using it. Instead, he was standing on tiptoes, anxiously looking this way and that over the tops of the dozens of heads milling around in all directions, trying to catch a glimpse of Judith.

Where was she?

As he continued to scan the crowded entrance hall, the general level of noise and laughter from the many people all around him seemed to swell; it boomed and reverberated, turning the hotel entrance into an echo chamber. There was still no sign of Judith, and Gerald was becoming frantic.

Suddenly, in the midst of the surrounding din, a consoling thought managed to fight its way through into his conscious mind, bringing him a moment of calm.

There's nothing to worry about.

She's just a few minutes late.

That's all.

Anyone can be running a little behind schedule.

Be patient.

Gerald glanced at his watch again.

It was 1.05pm.

OK, so she was only five minutes late – it might simply be due to nothing more than her watch not being set properly. Even now she might be parking the car and would be appearing through the revolving door imminently.

On the other hand, if there was a more serious reason for her lateness, she would probably have tried to call him in his room – and if he wasn't there he would miss her call. If he wasn't there, she might think he hadn't received her letter. Worse yet, if he wasn't there it might appear to her that he wasn't wanting to meet her at all.

With a final, unfruitful glance around the crowded foyer, Gerald turned and walked briskly back to the elevator, just in time to squeeze himself in with half a dozen sports team members, all of whom were in high spirits. In the confined space, their over-loud laughter and ceaseless chatter made Gerald feel ill, and he heaved a sigh of relief when the rowdy bunch finally exited on the tenth floor, leaving Gerald free to continue his upward journey alone.

When he at last reached his floor, he all but sprinted along the corridor.

While he had been downstairs and out of his suite, if Judith had tried to call, he told himself, she would have at least left a message on his voicemail.

Of course she would.

There was no need to panic.

Upon reaching his door, he fumbled with his key card as

he tried to push it into the narrow slot. After several attempts, the door finally swung, reluctantly, open.

Gerald hared into the room beyond and raced towards the phone on the desk. His heart skipped a beat. The message light was flashing! He grabbed the receiver and pushed the button. There was a series of electronic beeps and clicks, and a pre-recorded voice announced that he had a new message.

He could hardly breathe as he waited for the message to begin.

"This is the food and beverage manager speaking. We are pleased to advise that we have a special promotional offer on all in-room dining services this week…."

Gerald slammed the phone down and stared out through the window.

Where was she?

If it was simply the case that she was running late, as he had first supposed, then perhaps by now she may have arrived and would be waiting for him downstairs in the lobby after all.

Without a moment's pause, he raced out of the room, slamming the door behind him, and ran towards the elevator once again.

***

At 1.30 there was still no sign of her.

Gerald paced back and forth in the lavishly decorated hotel foyer, feeling frustrated and nervous. Occasionally, his aimless walking would attract a glance from one of the reception staff, or the concierge, but no one spoke to him.

2pm came and went.

And 2.30.

It was just after 3pm when Gerald, dejected and with

shoulders slumped, slowly returned to his room. There was still just the chance, he hoped, that a message – a real message this time – might be waiting for him, though by now he knew the chances of that were slim.

He was correct.

This time, the red light on the phone was not flashing.

There was no message.

Gerald sat down on the plush, luxurious sofa, alone, and put his head in his hands.

***

The next morning, the first thing he saw when he awoke was the empty whiskey bottle standing on the table next to his bed, with an empty glass alongside it.

Gerald groaned and rolled over. He couldn't remember drinking any whiskey at all, let alone finishing the bottle.

Eventually, he dragged himself from the bed, rubbed his eyes and began to stagger towards the bathroom. However, as he passed the open door to the living room, at the far end he could see that a piece of paper had been pushed under the door. Curious, he went and picked it up. It was an envelope from the desk of the concierge. Gerald opened it and removed the contents.

Although the message was short, Gerald felt his pulse quicken as he recognised the handwriting. He leant against the wall and began to read.

Dear Gerald,

I can only apologise for not keeping our appointment yesterday. Something urgent came up that required my immediate attention. I hope you understand.

I'm going to be busy today, but if you are free I could come and meet tomorrow? I can bring the children.

Best regards,
Judith.

As with her earlier messages, the word 'regards' still stung, but at least she had been in touch to explain her absence. As before, there was no phone number or any other means of contacting her, so Gerald was unable to reply. He was unable to say that of course he would be free tomorrow. Of course, he wanted his wife and children back. Of course, he wanted everything to get back on an even keel again.

So, she was coming tomorrow.

Good.

He would make sure he was ready.

Again.

***

The next night, Gerald sat alone at the table in his dining room. The remains of his half-eaten meal were pushed to one side, though the bottle of wine was already empty.

For the second time, Judith had not appeared.

And, therefore, neither had his children.

The television was on and he was staring at it, but taking nothing in.

Finally, his lip began to tremble, his eyes became glazed, and he began to weep.

***

Two years had now passed, yet the whole miserable experience had caused something to happen to Gerald.

Something had changed on the inside.

He had tried to deal with the situation, as best he could, but somewhere, deep down in the furthest recesses and corners of his mind, there was the faintest awareness that he was responding in a way which was not entirely rational.

He did know that.

He did.

Yet, somehow, not consciously enough.

Judith had said that she would come, and she had said so repeatedly.

The notes had continued to arrive, usually once every two to three weeks. In each one she apologised profusely for missing the preceding appointment and promised she would definitely be at the next one.

He wanted to believe that she still would.

He *had* to believe it.

Whatever else, Judith was an honest woman.

She was.

And, when she finally *did* arrive, she would be bringing the children with her. At least, that was what she kept hinting at. Maybe, after she and Gerald had chatted for a while, they would be able to resolve whatever needed resolving and resume the happy family life which had been going along so well before all this unpleasantness had arisen.

She had said she would come.

He knew she would.

Obviously, things kept happening to thwart her plans, but as soon as everything was sorted out, she would come.

She would.

And so, each morning, Gerald would come down to breakfast, request a table for four, and then place a glass of orange juice in each of the other three places.

Then, each lunchtime, he would do the same.

And again, when the dinner service began.

And, each time he finally rose from the table, alone, before returning to his suite he would first go to the lobby and wait there for a while, eagerly scanning the faces of everyone who was walking through or milling around, knowing that sooner or later his dear Judith would return to him.

She would.

Then, once he returned to his rooms for the night, he would first check to see whether the message light was flashing on the phone.

It wasn't. So he would simply sit and stare at it, willing the phone to ring, until he finally fell asleep.

Martha

With an old person's grunt and a sigh, dear Martha Higgins set down her china tea-cup with its matching saucer on the wide arm of her chair, next to her much-read bible, which was now very dog-eared and almost as old as she was. The cup rattled slightly against the silver plated teaspoon – a sound which Martha had always loved. She had never been able to understand how anyone could ever be satisfied with drinking tea from … from a *mug!* As far as she was concerned, there was only one way to fully appreciate the subtle qualities and characteristics of properly prepared tea. It simply had to be brewed in a pre-warmed china pot, and then poured into a china cup, before being sipped demurely – none of this gulping.

Glancing towards the window, she saw that the weather was not showing any signs of brightening up. It was still a grey, overcast, damp, miserable-looking day, and it was not inviting. She really didn't want to go out into what she knew would be a chilly temperature, especially since it would take her quite some time to don her coat, scarf, hat and gloves. Once that was accomplished she would then need to fetch her mobility scooter from the shed. That was always such a palaver, and the thought of having to trudge to the end of the back garden and wrestle with the stiff, unhelpful lock on the rickety shed door caused her to sigh again.

However, she knew that the expedition had to be made, because today was the day when she needed to collect her pension.

In the past, before she'd had to rely on her motorised scooter, she had always found the outing to be a pleasant one, since it was highly likely that she would meet familiar faces down at the post office, where even the cashier greeted her by name. Some time ago, though, due to 'cuts', her local post office had closed down, meaning that Martha now had to make a much longer journey down to the larger branch on the main High Street, and all those familiar faces from time gone by just didn't seem to be around anymore.

Of course, she had been given the option of having her pension paid directly into her bank – she still had the letter that explained how to arrange that somewhere – but that would have meant having to set up an account online, which was something the elderly lady simply didn't feel confident enough to attempt. So the High Street it had to be. Anyway, she told herself, to get out in the fresh air, even if it was rather cold, would do her good.

As a matter of course, she always waited until the afternoon to commence her journey, knowing that the Post Office was always especially busy on Monday mornings. That was the time when, it seemed, everyone who had any sort of financial benefit to collect, would all arrive at once – not only pensioners, but also numerous mothers with babies and toddlers, often bringing over-sized buggies which blocked the aisle, making it virtually impossible for anyone else to get in or out of the place.

So, towards the end of the afternoon was the preferred

time for her visit, and that time had finally come. Martha glanced longingly at her bible once again, which, with its many crimped and crumpled pages, lay open beside her. Today, her reading had been from the first chapter in the book of Joshua, which included the verse, *The Lord your God will be with you, wherever you go.* That was one of Martha's favourites. Years ago, she had committed it to memory but she still loved to read it in its context. She was about to pick up the old volume and read it again, but then she stopped herself. It will still be there when you come back, she said, under her breath. Realising that she could not put off the fateful moment any longer, Martha carefully placed her teacup on a side table and slowly raised herself from her comfy armchair. How she missed her younger days! Back then, she never moved slowly. As a professional dancer she had been supremely agile. Alas, that was no longer the case.

"Well, Lord," she said, under her breath, "Now I have to go out. Please help me to get there and back safely – and if you could keep the rain away until I've returned I would really appreciate it."

A few minutes later she was securely layered within her warm fleecy coat, while her thick scarf was wrapped snugly around her neck, and her imitation fur hat was placed atop her thinning grey hair. The gloves would have to wait until she had extracted her scooter from the shed, as there was no way she could manage to turn the key in the lock whilst wearing such thick hand protectors.

After reaching the back door, and bracing herself for the blast of cold air from the garden that she knew was waiting for her, she unlocked and opened it. Such was the severity of the chill that she gave an involuntary gasp as the cold air reached the back of her throat. A little gingerly, Martha then stepped out of the door, locking it carefully behind her, and descended the three steps to her garden path. Making her way along the cracked crazy paving, she sighed at the sight of the barren flowerbeds. In the past, back when she had had the strength to tend her garden, these had been a mass of bloom, a delight to the eye. Sadly, those days were now long gone. A few isolated brown, lifeless stems fought to hold their place as they protruded up, stoically, through the tough, tightly packed soil, and that was all.

Martha reached the end of the garden and opened her purse. She placed the back door key safely inside, and took out the key to the shed. She already knew that opening the shed door would be a struggle – it had never been easy – yet this occasion seemed to be even more difficult than usual. With all this recent cold, damp weather, perhaps the door's wooden panels had expanded.

With an effort, Martha persevered. The reluctant lock finally admitted defeat, and a grating click announced that the shed door had at last yielded to her wishes.

Trying to coax the mobility scooter from the shed was always a laborious process, and Martha often found herself wondering at this situation which did present her with something of a paradox: on the one hand, manoeuvring this cumbersome and unwieldy machine was a real effort which often left her exhausted and gasping for breath. On the other hand, the whole point of having this blasted scooter was to make her life easier!

However, practical difficulties aside, Martha was actually very grateful for this mode of transport. Since its arrival, courtesy of her two grown-up children who had offered to share the cost between them, she no longer felt herself to be a prisoner in her own home. She had been able to be much more active, going to the nearby shops, visiting the park, and meeting up with her friends at the fortnightly coffee morning in the local church hall. Plus, on pension day, it meant that she was able to go and collect her money without having to wait for a bus, or ask her neighbour for a lift.

With a certain amount of heaving and straining, none of which was even remotely ladylike, Martha finally managed to drag the machine from the shed. After placing her purse and shopping bag in the little basket attached to the front, she then trundled the scooter the short distance to the back gate. She opened it, and paused for a moment to catch her breath.

The gate opened onto a narrow alleyway that ran along the back of the row of terraced houses. As a thoroughfare, it could hardly be described as a pleasant one, being lined with what seemed like an interminable line of dustbins. Whilst these obstacles did narrow the passageway quite significantly, Martha relished the challenge that they placed upon her driving skills; she felt quite proud that she was able to navigate her way around and through them without too much difficulty.

However, on this occasion her control of the scooter, and her reflexes, underwent a severe test. She had almost reached the end of the alleyway when, without warning, she was startled by a young man who suddenly appeared, coming from the opposite direction. Martha let out a scream. She tried to steer clear, but in the heat of the moment she turned the wrong way and almost ran straight into him.

"Hey, watch it, Missus!" the denim-clad pedestrian exclaimed, as he leapt nimbly to one side, just in the nick of time.

The scooter bumped into one of the tall wheelie bins, causing it to topple over and spew its contents in all directions, before finally lurching to a halt.

"Oh dear," Martha whimpered. "I'm so sorry. Are you all right?"

"No bones broken," came the reply, along with an impish

grin, "but are you OK? You look a bit rattled."

"Oh, yes, thank you. I'm quite fine. Yes. Really. Fine. Quite fine."

"Glad to hear that. Here, let me help separate you from that bin."

"Oh, please don't worry. I'm sure I can manage."

"Hmm … I don't think so."

Martha glanced down and saw that the front wheel of her mobility scooter had somehow become wedged inside the handle of the upturned garbage receptacle, which was now lying on its side, while the rubbish from within now lay strewn across the alley. Still in her seat, she attempted to jostle the wheel free, but to no avail.

"Well," she said, "perhaps I do need your help after all – just a little."

She gave a slight smile, feeling somewhat sheepish about the whole incident.

"It'll be easier if you get off the scooter first."

"Oh, yes, of course."

Martha shuffled out of the seat and stepped away from the machine.

The young man bent down, grabbed the scooter's front wheel in one hand and the edge of the bin in the other. He gave a firm tug and a little twist, and the wheel came free.

"There ya go!" he announced.

"Thank you," said Martha. "Please accept my apologies. I really didn't intend to run you over."

"Don't mention it," the young fellow replied. "No harm done. Let me hold it steady while you get back on."

"Oh, thank you. That's really most kind."

A few moments later found the scooter's owner back in the saddle and ready to be on her way once again.

"Mind how you go," said the young man. He then raised a warning finger, adding, "and no speeding."

"I don't think there's much chance of that," said Martha, giving a sweet little old lady's giggle. "According to the manual, these machines have a top speed of only six miles per hour, and that's quite fast enough for me."

She smiled again at the young fellow and began to drive away. However, only a few moments later, and before she had reached the corner where she would turn onto the main pavement, she heard some raised voices behind her. She slowed to a halt and looked back over her shoulder. The young man who had helped her was still standing there, but now he had been joined by another man. Had this new arrival been one of her neighbours, Martha would have recognised him straight away, but she knew she had never seen him before.

The two figures contrasted strikingly with each other. This new arrival was noticeably taller and somewhat older than the first man, and he was a snappy dresser, wearing a suit that fitted well and was clearly of good quality – probably tailor-made, Martha thought.

The two of them were involved in a heated discussion.

"Are you saying I'm a thief? Is that what you're saying?" the young man shouted.

"If you are not, then tell me where you got that purse."

"I've already told you. I found it lying here – not that it's any business of yours – and I was just about to go and hand it in at the police station."

"Actually, there is no need to go to all that trouble. The lady who lost it is right there."

The taller man turned and pointed straight at Martha.

Taken a little aback at this revelation, Martha glanced into the basket on the front of her scooter. Sure enough, although her shopping bag was still there, her purse was not. She fixed the young man with an icy stare.

In an instant, the young man suddenly turned and began

to run in the opposite direction, but he was not quick enough. The older man was surprisingly agile and grabbed the youth, spinning him round and holding him in an arm-lock.

"Hey, let me go! You're hurting me," he yelled.

He continued to struggle and curse, but was unable to prevent the older man from propelling him over to where Martha still sat on her mobility scooter.

"Now then," he said. "I'm sure that if you just give the purse back to the nice lady we can put this whole unfortunate business behind us."

As he spoke he gave the young lad's arm another twist, making him wince.

"Ow! Let me go. I wasn't stealing it. I found it lying on the ground and was going to hand it in."

"Hmm. I hope you'll forgive me for not believing you." Another twist of the arm. "Now, why don't you give the lady her purse?"

With his one free arm, the shamefaced lad handed it over. Martha nodded.

"Thank you," she said.

As the older man released his grip, the young lad sprinted away, running at top speed along the alley, before disappearing from sight as he rounded the corner at the far end.

Martha watched him go, in reflective mood.

"He seemed like such a nice young man," she said.

"Can't be too careful," the older man said. "Are you OK?"

"Yes, I'm fine," Martha replied. She paused for a moment, looking along the alley in the direction the young man had gone. Then she began to speak again.

"Incidentally," she said, as she turned back to the tall man again – and then she stopped, surprised.

The man had completely disappeared.

Martha looked up and down the alleyway, and glanced into all the back gardens within sight, but there was no sign of him. There was nowhere he could have gone without her seeing him depart, so where on earth was he? Where had he gone? Martha was dumbfounded.

After a few moments, she shrugged. Obviously, he was a faster mover than Martha had realised. Feeling thankful for the man's timely intervention, she placed her purse back in the basket, but this time made a point of placing it under the shopping bag so that it was out of sight.

Then she re-commenced her journey to the post office to collect her pension.

***

It was some time later when Martha returned home and, after going through the usual ordeal of heaving the scooter back into the shed, she re-entered her home and put the kettle on.

Martha was naturally careful with her money. Hers was a generation that always watched how every penny was spent. However, on this occasion, while she had been out she had allowed herself one small indulgence: on her way home she had popped into the local family bakery – an establishment that she loved, where all its wares were baked on the premises, and which always gave forth such a delightful aroma – and treated herself to a slice of her favourite deliciously succulent Dundee cake.

Once the tea was brewing in her favourite china pot, she placed it on a tray, together with her china cup and saucer. Finally, the newly purchased cake was added, on a matching china plate of its own, and she carried the whole tasteful arrangement through into her living room, where her comfy chair was waiting for her, along with her bible which she had left open on the arm of the chair.

She had already taken a few sips of tea, and had begun to nibble her way through the slice of cake, when something caught her eye which surprised her. She was sure that she had left it open at the book of Joshua, where her favourite verse of scripture was located. Yet now it was lying open at the book of Proverbs.

While Martha was pondering this, her gaze fell upon the words of chapter 15, verse 3. As she read, her mouth fell open.

The eyes of the Lord are everywhere, keeping watch on the wicked and the good.

Setting her tea and cake back on the tray, she picked up the weighty old volume, and was about to turn back to the book of Joshua but, as she began to turn the pages, they fell open at Psalm 121 and the words of verse 8 leapt up at her.

The Lord will watch over your coming and going, both now and forevermore.

Martha exhaled deeply and sat back in her chair, allowing the words she had just read to sink in.

Who was that tall man who had appeared from nowhere, and disappeared again just as quickly? His arrival was certainly timely – there was no denying that.

Surely not.

It couldn't have really been *him* … could it?

Could it?

Owen

The disease finally came to an end.

Owen died, at last, after a long illness, patiently borne.

He hadn't wanted to die. Not at all. He was still young, and there was so much he had still wanted to do. However, he resigned himself to the inevitable once he made the solemn discovery that he didn't really have any say in the matter.

Family members had been called, and, despite the fact that Owen and his wife lived in a remote rural area, most had been able to respond to the summons. They were now gathered round the bed, with heads bowed. Some were sobbing, quietly, into handkerchiefs, while others placed a comforting hand on the arm or shoulder of a loved one.

A doctor was also in attendance, though, apart from trying to make the final moments as comfortable as possible, everyone knew there was not really anything he could do.

And the local priest was there too, a calming presence in the otherwise tense atmosphere of the room. He stood, respectfully, in the corner of the room. Sometimes he was silent; sometimes he was praying softly; at one point he quietly recited the words of the twenty-third psalm.

A variety of candles had been placed at intervals around the room. Several of these had begun to sputter and spark, as the molten wax began to encroach upon the slowly shortening wick.

It was in in the centre of this peaceful and respectful gathering that Owen's final moments were reached, and he quietly slipped away. It happened so gently, and so inconspicuously, that it took an appreciable number of moments for people to realise that he was, in fact, no longer breathing.

Owen was pleased – yes, pleased – to discover that the actual moment of death was simple and quick, and it wasn't painful at all.

For a second, nothing happened.

Then, suddenly, he was free.

He stood, looking down at his motionless corpse and at all the grim faced relatives. Then he reached out and placed a hand on the shoulders of his daughter. It seemed that perhaps she was aware of it, because she looked up at that moment. Owen smiled down at her, but his smile was not returned. Instead, the beautiful little girl began to sob, and those alongside tried to comfort her.

As he gazed down upon the sorry scene, Owen suddenly knew that he did not wish to be present in this unhappy place any longer.

What about that lovely summer's day they had all spent at the beach? He wanted to be there. Why *couldn't* he be there?

Just then, there was a bright flash from somewhere. It was multi-coloured and garish, and Owen shielded his eyes. Then, he opened them again and suddenly, all at once, he *was* there – at the beach.

He didn't like it.

It was deserted and desolate, and nothing like the thriving, bustling place he remembered.

The sound of the waves washing up on the shore sounded deeply sorrowful, and the screeching of a seagull overhead cut through the icy wind like a sharp knife.

Feeling morose, he began to take a few steps in the soft sand, but then the sudden flash came again.

This time, when he opened his eyes he was standing in a church.

About half the pews were occupied, with people who all looked sad.

At the far end, in front of the altar, Owen saw a coffin and realised, with a start, that he was witnessing his own funeral.

He walked slowly down the centre aisle, looking left and right at all those in attendance as they did their best to sing a mournful hymn. Most of them were family and friends. He smiled at them and raised his hand in greeting, but it seemed that they did not see him. Some of his neighbours were there too, as was his doctor, and there were a handful of others who he didn't recognise at all.

He reached the front and, approaching the coffin, he gazed down at the simple yet tasteful wreath that adorned it. Then he noticed the brass plate attached to the top. His name had been engraved upon it and, just beneath, the dates on which his life had begun and ended.

Young.

He had been too young to go.

It wasn't his time, and he wasn't ready.

The hymn ended and the vicar stood up to deliver the eulogy. Owen took a step forward, interested to hear what would be said, but then the sudden flash came once more, and everything around him dissolved into a kaleidoscope of spinning shapes and colours.

This time, when Owen opened his eyes he found he was at the funeral reception. He recognised the venue straight away; it was the function room on the first floor of his favourite pub. Some people were standing, while others were sitting. Some were chatting; others were silent. All were holding a paper plate with a selection of triangular sandwiches with the crusts cut off, a sausage roll and a slice of quiche, together with a drink in a plastic cup. Owen had always been amazed at the way human beings managed to eat or drink anything whilst holding a full plate in one hand and a drink in the other, but it seemed to be an inherited skill.

Owen approached the bar and reached towards a bowl of peanuts, but his fingers went right through and he found that he was unable to pick them up. Surprised, he tried again. He looked firstly at his hand. It seemed solid enough. He then reached towards the bowl but, as he brought his fingertips together, rather than being able to pick up some of the peanuts as he intended, his fingers instead sank into them before reappearing from out the other side. He could not feel them, and they did not move at his touch.

Behind the counter, a bored bartender stood with arms folded. He was looking in Owen's direction but he did not see him. Alcoholic drinks were available but everyone was opting, instead, for the complimentary fruit juice, serving themselves from the glass jugs that had been placed on the rickety trestle tables alongside the various plates of snacks.

Against one wall, a complicated-looking fruit machine flashed its lights madly, and glared at all present, trying its best to tempt them into inserting some coins into its ever hungry slot, but everyone ignored it.

At one end of the room, Owen saw his wife, standing with their three year-old little girl. The uncooperative bowl of peanuts was forgotten as he smiled and moved towards them. They both looked pensive and sad, yet composed, as they stood next to a table upon which was an open book of blank pages. Guests had formed a short queue and, in turn, after speaking a few comforting words to his wife and child, then picked up a pen and wrote something in the book of condolence before moving away again.

Owen drew near and listened to some of the things being said.

"We are deeply sorry for your loss."

"Owen was a good friend. He'll be missed."

"I was looking forward to trouncing him at our next quiz night."

As he stood, listening, something caught Owen's attention and he glanced over to the far corner of the room to see his doctor sitting there. He was talking, but he appeared decidedly ill-at-ease, while his wife sat alongside and placed her hand on his arm to comfort him. Feeling curious, Owen began to make his way towards them. As he drew near, the words began to become audible above the surrounding general hubbub.

"I could have done more. I *should* have done more."

"Don't blame yourself, darling. You did everything you could."

The doctor gave a rueful smile.

"I appreciate your confidence," he said, "but in fact I did not do everything."

A puzzled look crossed his wife's face.

"Whatever do you mean?" she asked.

"I knew what medicine he needed," he said, looking down at the floor, "but I had only a little left. More was ordered, but it did not arrive in time."

His wife leant towards him and spoke softly.

Owen leaned closer too.

"Are you saying," she whispered, "that if you had given

him the little medicine you had, Owen would still be alive?"

The doctor lifted his head, looked into the eyes of his wife, and gave a sad, almost imperceptible nod.

"No!" Owen screamed, at the top of his voice, though no one heard him.

He ran towards the bar where a row of newly washed wine glasses had been lined up. In a blinding rage, he swung an arm to swipe them aside – but they all remained, motionless, in their places as his violent limb swept through, unperturbed by his distress. Owen staggered, holding his hands to his head. Then he looked around at the other guests who, it seemed, had now lost all sense of the solemnity of the occasion; they were laughing and joking together, and turning what should have been a serious gathering into nothing more than a jolly party.

In anger and frustration, he turned and ran from the room. As he reached the wooden door he so much wanted to slam it behind him, louder than he had ever done, but he now knew it would be futile to even try.

And yet, as he drew near, and even though he knew it was a useless gesture, the resentment and sheer vexation within caused him to reach out for it – and, to his complete surprise, this time he felt his fingers close around the edge of the solid oak door. He stepped through the door and, before he quite realised what he was doing, pulled on it with all his strength, slamming it shut with such force that the frame shook and shards of plaster fell from the ceiling above.

All conversation in the room ceased abruptly as every head turned towards the cacophonous sound and the now closed door. For a few seconds, the door remained closed, but there must have been some mis-alignment between the door and its frame for, a moment later, it slowly began to swing open once more. The people gathered there could see the passageway beyond, but not its occupant.

Owen stood there, glaring back into the room at the sea of startled faces, and at the doctor in particular. Then, just as suddenly as before, there came again the intensely bright flash of light. Owen closed his eyes as he vanished from the scene.

***

When he opened his eyes again, Owen found that he was back at the beach.

The tide was out, and the gently undulating sand seemed to stretch for miles towards the faraway ocean, which could be seen as a thin, grey line in the distance.

Although all was calm around him, inside his earlier feelings of sadness and disappointment were now mixed with annoyance and deep resentment, creating a seething caution of jumbled emotions which threatened to tear him apart.

His doctor hadn't given him the medicine he needed!

Why?

WHY?

Tears, a blend of anger and deep unhappiness, began coursing down his sallow cheeks as he tried to assimilate all that had happened. It was some time before he became conscious of the fact that he was now sitting on the sand. He couldn't remember sitting down, so he was slightly surprised by this realisation. What surprised him even more, however, was the observation that he was running his fingers through the sand, and that the sand was actually behaving as it should. He paused, and tried again, grabbing a handful of the fine grains and holding them aloft, before opening his fingers slightly, allowing the sand to slip between them and be blown along on the light breeze.

Earlier, he had not been able to grasp solid objects, but now he found that he could.

He had also thought that when the mysterious flash occurred, the place to which he was transported was somehow selected at random. Yet now he realised that he had the ability to select where he went, and that each place he had visited so far had been the result of – not so much a choice on his part – but more of a *desire*.

In the distance he could see the pier. During the summer months it was always bustling with tourists, crowding around the various stalls and kiosks, but now it stood empty.

Owen closed his eyes and concentrated.

Then, a moment later, still with his eyes closed, he knew – somehow, he just *knew* – that he was now standing on the pier. Slowly, he opened his eyes and found that, in an instant, he had indeed moved from the beach to the pier.

He smiled to himself. It was a grim smile.

It was time to have some fun.

Or, perhaps, not really fun.

A better word would be *revenge*.

***

The three year-old girl lay in her cot, sleeping peacefully.

Standing over her, Owen stood in the darkened room looking down at his daughter, a tear trickling slowly down his cheek.

"I'm sorry," he whispered. "I'm so, so sorry."

He didn't want to leave. He wanted to stay there forever with his beautiful angel.

Yet he knew he could not and, at length, he finally managed to turn away.

Without opening it, he walked through the door into the adjoining bedroom where his dear wife was also asleep. She had drifted into slumber still clutching a photograph of herself and Owen, which had been taken on their wedding day.

Owen leant forward and gently stroked her lovely face. She stirred slightly, but did not awaken.

"Please forgive me," said Owen. "It was not my fault. I did not leave; I was taken from you."

Suddenly, his wife's eyes opened and she sat bolt upright.

"Owen?" she said, speaking into the darkness. "Owen?"

"Yes, yes, my love, I'm here," he called, and stooped to embrace her.

She felt nothing as his arms went straight through her, and Owen cried out in frustration.

He paused, and concentrated hard, knowing that if he were able to direct the power of his emotions he would have a far greater chance of being able to interact with the natural world. Breathing slowly and deeply, he reached out to his wife again. This time he could feel her. He could feel her soft skin and the folds of her silk night dress. He could feel her breath as his fingers went by her mouth and nose, and he found that he could smell her perfume – the perfume he had given her on their last anniversary.

He could feel her.

But, beyond the merest hint of a current of air in the otherwise still room, she felt nothing.

"Owen?" she said, again, into the silence, but then she gave out a long sigh. "Oh, Owen … I thought, for just a moment … I thought…."

She took a deep breath, then spoke aloud to herself in the darkness of the room.

"Only to be expected, I suppose. Come on, girl, get some rest." She lay down once more, and pulled the covers about her. "It was just a dream," she whispered, as sleep began to take her. "But what a lovely, lovely dream." She clutched the photo again and held it against her bosom. "I shall miss you, darling, very much. Darling Owen…."

Her eyes closed.

Owen felt his heart would break.

"Don't worry, my dearest," he said. "I am going to set things straight, you'll see." He spoke sadly, knowing she had not heard him, as he began to fade from the room.

***

Barely an instant later, Owen found himself standing in another bedroom. In many ways it was not dissimilar from the one he had just left. The curtains were drawn and there was a comfortable bed, along with a wardrobe and chest of drawers, and a dressing table.

The difference, though, lay with the occupants of the room.

The doctor and his wife were lying, close together and fast asleep.

Owen looked down at them, his face serious.

"You took me from my family," he hissed. "You had the medicine I needed. Why didn't you give it to me?"

The doctor was suddenly awake and he sat up. He was staring straight ahead, wide-eyed, into the darkness, and he was sweating. The abruptness of his movement caused his wife to open her eyes.

"Are you all right?" she asked. "What's the matter?"

"Did you hear something?" he asked.

His wife paused, listening.

"No," she said, "I didn't, and I can't hear anything now. Did you have another of your bad dreams?"

"I … I don't know. I don't think so. Maybe. Oh, I don't know."

"Hush, now," she said. "Come back to sleep." As she

spoke, his wife reached up and placed a hand on his shoulder. Her husband sighed.

"Yes, my dear," he said. "All right."

He laid himself down again and, beneath the covers, reached out to put an arm around his wife. At that moment, he heard a creaking sound.

It was there. Right there in the room, with them.

Neither of them moved.

"Did you hear that?" he whispered.

"Yes," his wife replied. "I did."

They lay in the bed, motionless, straining their ears into the darkness for the slightest hint of any further sound.

There was nothing.

"I'm going to switch on the light," said the doctor.

He reached out to the lamp that stood on his bedside table and, a moment later, a glow of soft light filled the room. He gasped.

The wardrobe door was standing open.

"How on earth did that happen?" he asked.

"I've no idea," his wife answered. "It hasn't happened before."

"Back to sleep," he said. "I'll take a look at the hinges in the morning."

As he was reaching for the light switch, the creaking sound was heard again.

And this time the doctor and his wife both saw it.

The wardrobe door moved.

And then it moved again.

"What's happening?" his wife whimpered.

"Don't worry," said the doctor. "I'm sure there's a perfectly rational explanation."

Owen sniggered as he swung the door back and forth, with increasing rapidity.

Then he reached inside and began to take out all the

clothes. At first, he simply dropped them on the floor, but as he continued he realised it would be much more fun to hurl them around the room.

The doctor's wife began to cry, and she clung to her husband in desperation as one garment after another left the wardrobe and flew out into the room.

"Darling, what is going on?" she wailed.

The doctor didn't reply, but held his wife, tightly.

"I'll tell you what's going on," yelled Owen, even though he knew they wouldn't hear him. "Were it not for you, my wife would still have a husband, and my daughter would still have a father!"

As he spoke, he slammed the wardrobe door as hard as he could, and then, reaching behind it, gave a sharp tug, sending the whole thing toppling to the floor, where it landed with a loud crash.

The doctor's wife screamed.

Owen chuckled.

At that moment, he was startled as he suddenly became aware of another presence in the room.

He glanced round to see a wide circle of light which appeared to be hovering and oscillating in mid-air. It had no clear form, and its edges were indistinct, yet somehow Owen knew that this was a sentient being.

"Who are you?" Owen demanded. "What do you want?"

The light did not answer either question but responded with one of its own.

"What are you doing here, Owen?"

"I wouldn't be here at all if it wasn't for him." Owen pointed at the doctor as he spoke. "He deserves what he's getting and he's brought it all on himself."

"Why are you so angry?"

"How can you ask such a stupid question?" Owen railed. "This so called doctor, whose job is to take care of me, didn't give me the treatment he knew I needed. Did you hear me? He *knew* what was needed and he didn't do it."

As he spoke, his gaze fell upon a row of framed family photographs which had been arranged on a shelf. The people in the photos were all smiling, happy and contented.

"Look!" yelled Owen, gesturing towards the pictures. "He still has his family. Well, what about mine? What about my family, the family *he* ripped apart!"

With that, he swung an arm and swiped the whole collection onto the floor, where they fell with a loud clatter. The doctor and his wife clung to each other in the bed. They were now both in tears and too terrified to move.

"You're quite right."

These words of agreement from the hovering light, spoken softly yet firmly, caught Owen off guard, and he found himself somewhat taken aback. He felt as though he wanted to reply, and he did indeed try to gather his thoughts, but no words came.

"Yes," the voice continued, "your doctor did know what medicine you needed, and it is true that he decided not to give it to you. However, when the situation is viewed from all angles, the person here who has made the error is you."

"Me? *Me?* Are you saying this is all *my* fault?"

Once again, the voice did not answer directly.

"Do you see that door, over there?" the voice asked.

Owen glanced across the room.

"Of course I do. What about it?"

"There is something in the room beyond which might be of interest to you, but we will come to that shortly. For now, I will just say this: you left your funeral reception too soon." There was a short pause. It almost felt as though the light was considering something. Then it spoke again. "It would be good for you to return there, for a moment."

Before Owen could reply there came again the now

familiar flash, together with all the twirling colours, and then, all at once, he was back – back there at his reception, standing and looking down at the doctor and his wife who were sitting and talking quietly, though the circle of light was now nowhere to be seen.

As before, Owen drew near, and listened.

"I could have done more. I *should* have done more."

"Don't blame yourself, darling. You did everything you could."

"I appreciate your confidence, but in fact I did not do everything."

"Whatever do you mean?"

"I knew what medicine he needed, but I had only a little left. More was ordered, but it did not arrive in time."

"Are you saying, that if you had given him the little medicine you had, Owen would still be alive?"

"Yes. Yes, *he* would, but our little girl would not be. I only had enough for one dose. I had to give it to her. What other choice could I make?"

As he heard the doctor's words, Owen staggered back, holding his hands to his head.

There was a flash as the twisting vortex reappeared and, an instant later, Owen was back in the bedroom, where the doctor and his wife were still holding tightly to one another. The circle of light was hovering but said nothing. There was a click and the door to the adjoining room opened. A little girl, of about four years old, came running in.

"Mummy, daddy," she said, "I'm frightened. There was a lot of noise and it woke me up."

She clambered up onto the bed, crawled between her parents and snuggled down under the blankets. Only then did she register all the chaos in the room.

"Oh," she exclaimed, "look at all this mess! What happened?"

The voice from the light now spoke again.

"Did your doctor make the right choice, Owen? In the circumstances, what was the correct thing for him to do? Had you been in his position, what would *you* have done?"

Owen looked around the room, at all the carnage he had wreaked. He looked at the doctor and his wife, still frightened, holding onto each other while trying to remain calm and reassure their young daughter.

This time, he spoke much more quietly.

"What will happen to my family?" he asked.

"You don't need to worry about them. They'll be all right."

"They'll be all right?" Owen felt his feelings of frustration begin to rise again. "They'll be all right? And that's it? My family suffers irreparable damage, while this so-called doctor and his family get to spend all their lives together? Is nothing going to happen to him? Does he just get away with it?"

"Owen, Owen." The tone of the voice was calm and reassuring. "He found himself in a position where he had to make a choice. It was a choice he absolutely did not want to make, but he was forced to do so. He made his decision, and the fallout will be on his conscience for the rest of his life. Surely that is punishment enough?"

Owen exhaled slowly and loudly, and looked back towards the bed once more. This time, as he looked upon the scared, huddled family, he felt only pity. Then, in the midst of all the fallen debris, he saw again the selection of photos littering the floor, and one in particular caught his attention. Although the wooden frame was dented, and the glass was now cracked, the picture itself was still clear: it showed the doctor and his wife, sitting in the garden with their beautiful little girl. They were all smiling at one another and the sun was shining. It was a lovely photo; there was no question about that. Owen bent down and picked it up.

From where they sat in the bed, the frightened family felt another surge of fear as the photo, apparently of its own volition, lifted itself from the floor. It appeared to hover in mid-air as, one by one, the splintered shards of glass that still clung to the frame were removed. Then it floated back towards the shelf where it had stood until a short time ago and gently settled itself back into its original place.

Owen removed his hand from the photo and stood back.

"You said my family would be OK," he said to the circle of light, "but what about them?" He looked back towards the doctor and his family. "Will they be OK too?"

"Yes," the voice replied. "They will, in due time."

"So what happens now?" Owen asked. "I mean, what happens to me?"

This time, the voice did not reply. Instead, it began to rise. As it did so, Owen felt himself being drawn upwards after it. He knew he had no choice but to follow, but he felt no urge to resist; he was quite happy to go along with it.

Leaving the doctor, his wife and their daughter, Owen rose up through the ceiling, out through the roof and into the night beyond. He floated along, slowly and gently. It almost felt as though the guiding light was giving him time to learn to feel at ease with this new means of movement. Still led by the bobbing circle of illumination, he noticed he was now being drawn towards his own house. A few moments later, he found himself inside. There was his little girl, fast asleep, at peace and beautiful, and his wife also slept, with a gentle smile on her lovely face.

He wanted to stay, to stay and gaze upon their serene beauty forever, but he knew it was time to go.

With a feeling of contentment, Owen turned to face the light again.

"I'm ready," he said.

Once more, the light drew him aloft. Owen rose higher

and higher, and, as he did so, he began to move faster and ever faster. The further he travelled, the more the darkness of the night receded, to be replaced by an ever-growing brightness, which gradually became one with the circle that guided him, as he hastened towards the awaiting future in his glorious new heavenly home.

Ricarda & Samuel

It was difficult to pinpoint exactly what it was about going to Grandpa's house that made it so enjoyable. Yet, for both Ricarda and her younger brother, Samuel, whenever they went to visit him, life just seemed to feel a bit more … well, special.

Now, as they sat in the car on the way to see their elderly relative, they could scarcely contain their excitement. This was because, unlike previous visits, on this occasion they weren't just going for an hour or two, where they would be back home again in time for dinner. No, *this* time they would be staying for the whole weekend, and they couldn't wait to get there.

"Now, children," said Mother, swivelling round to speak to them from the front passenger seat, "when we arrive don't get too excited. Grandpa is very much looking forward to seeing you, but do remember he doesn't have as much energy as you two. He needs to take several rests during the day, so make sure you don't wear him out."

Ricarda laughed. "Of course not, Mummy. We'll take great care of him, won't we Samuel?"

The little boy did not reply. Instead, he gave a mischievous giggle before turning away to look out of the window at the rural scenery which was speeding past.

"And then," Mother continued, "Daddy and I will be back to pick you up tomorrow evening."

***

If truth be told, though, Grandpa was even more excited at the prospect of seeing his grandchildren than they were at seeing him. Yes, he would certainly need to take care and pace himself, but he had been looking forward to this weekend for months, and had every intention of enjoying it to the full.

He had gone to great lengths to prepare for this visit: first, he had tidied up the garden, sweeping away the fallen leaves, and mowing the lawn, before wiping the accumulated dust and dirt from the climbing frame, slide and the garden chairs. He had also obtained a long piece of thick rope, which he fastened to the overhanging bough of a large oak tree to make a swing for the children to play on. Then, back inside the house, he had climbed up to the attic and brought down a selection of board games, placing them in a neat pile by the coffee table in the living room. Finally, he had made all the necessary preparations for 'the chocolate hunt' by hiding a large number of mini-sized chocolate bars all over the house. This particular game had become progressively more difficult to arrange since, with each successive visit, his grandchildren had become increasingly familiar with the places where all these delicious pieces of confectionery were likely to be hidden, so Grandpa now found that he was starting to run out of ideas for new hiding places. Still, having employed a little ingenuity, after a while they were all suitably concealed.

At least, he hoped so. He didn't want the hunt to be *too* easy.

The top prize in this particular search for chocolate was special indeed.

Many years ago, on his travels through Turkey, Grandpa had been browsing in a local craft market, and, on a certain stall, had discovered a very ornate, handmade wooden box, in the shape of an old fashioned treasure chest. It looked like something straight from a novel by Robert Louis Stevenson, and Grandpa had bought it immediately. Now, each time his grandchildren were due to visit, he would fill it with as many chocolate coins as he could, and hide it in an extra special place. When its location was finally discovered (as it always was, eventually) they would all sit down together and have a very unhealthy, but very enjoyable, feast.

"But don't tell your mother," Grandpa would say. "She told me I'm only allowed to give you one piece of candy at a time."

"Of course, Grandpa," Ricarda would reply, giggling through a mouthful of half-chewed chocolate. "We won't say a word."

Samuel often wouldn't reply at all, since he would have somehow managed to cram his mouth with even more chocolate than his sister, and was unable to speak, but he would nod his head in enthusiastic agreement.

"So we have a deal, then," Grandpa would say. "Yes, since you managed to find this pirate treasure all by yourselves I think you've earned your reward."

***

At last, the moment of arrival came.

With laughter and shouting, Ricarda and Samuel jumped out of the car, pushed open the garden gate, then came bounding along the path and up the stairs to the porch, where grandpa stood waiting, with arms outstretched.

After all the enthusiastic greetings and exchange of cuddles, Grandpa announced, "the games are waiting for you in the living room."

The two children went running into the house, shrieking with delight, as Grandpa turned to face his daughter who, together with his son-in-law, stood on the steps, smiling.

"They've really been looking forward to this," she said.

"So have I," he replied.

"Please don't give them too much chocolate."

Grandpa winked.

"As if I would," he said.

This provoked a roll of the eyes.

"Anyway, we'll be back to collect them tomorrow evening."

"No problem. You deserve some time to yourselves. Off you go and enjoy it."

Grandpa stood waving, as the car pulled away and disappeared round the corner at the end of the street. Then he turned and walked back into the house, where something of a surprise awaited him.

Ricarda and Samuel were in the living room, standing next to the pile of games, but hadn't touched any of them.

"Right," said Grandpa, "which game shall we play first?"

"Actually, Grandpa," said Ricarda, "we'd like you to tell us a story, wouldn't we, Samuel?"

Samuel nodded with enthusiasm, while Grandpa's eyes rose.

"Well, of course, if that's what you'd like."

"But please can we have the story in your reading room?"

"Of course you can. That's the perfect place for storytelling."

The two little people cheered, and immediately ran from

the room, heading towards the delights of their grandfather's literary emporium.

"Come on, Grandpa," they called as they scampered along.

By the time Grandpa reached the reading room, Ricarda and Samuel had already climbed up and squeezed themselves into his rocking chair. Sitting side by side, they rocked back and forth, smiling.

The reading room was Grandpa's favourite room in the whole house. It was characterful, with quaint lattice windows, and it was very cosy, containing an overstuffed sofa and two comfortable armchairs. There was a large, open fireplace, though this was only used during the cold months of the year. The soulful, resonant ticking of an impressive grandfather clock, which stood against the wall watching over the activities in the room, leant an atmosphere of stillness and calm.

Grandpa's rocking chair was positioned in front of a bookcase which was very old, and very large. Many years ago, the edges of the oaken shelves had been beautifully carved. The workmanship was exquisite and it had clearly been undertaken by a master of his craft. The bookcase itself was virtually bursting with books. Many were arranged neatly, in orderly rows, but others were just lying flat in piles at shelf endings, acting as makeshift bookends, while still others had been stuffed in horizontally, in the space just below the shelf above.

"Well, children," said Grandpa, "which story would you like?" He stood, with hands on hips, and surveyed the substantial collection. "How about this one?" he asked, pulling it from the shelf. "It's an exciting adventure story called *A Looming of Vultures*."

Ricarda shook her head, and Grandpa returned the book to its place.

"All right. What about this? This is a funny story about an under-appreciated music teacher called Godfrey Plunkett. No? Well, would you rather hear a tale of mystery? This one is a wonderful treasure hunt called *The Cryptic Lines*."

Then Samuel spoke up.

"Grandpa," he said, "please will you tell us a story from *The Book of Names*?"

"*The Book of Names?*" Grandpa repeated. "What do you think about that, Ricarda? Would you like a story from that book too?"

He smiled as he spoke, looking down at his two grandchildren, who sat, beaming up at him and nodding, as they swung forward and backward in his rocking chair.

"Very well," he said. "*The Book of Names* it is."

He reached out and pulled the requested tome from its place on the shelf.

"Now then," he said, "where is Grandpa supposed to sit?"

"Here, Grandpa, sit here!" cried Ricarda. She leapt from the chair and all but pulled the reluctant Samuel after her.

Grandpa sat down and then lifted the two youngsters up onto his knees, wrapping his arms around them. Holding *The Book of Names* in front, he opened the cover and turned to the contents page.

"Well now," he said, "which story would you like? We must choose carefully."

"Why, Grandpa?" Ricarda asked.

"Why? Well, because some of the stories in this book were written for grown-ups."

"Oh." Ricarda considered, holding a finger to her lips as she thought.

"But don't worry," said Grandpa. "There are plenty of other tales in here which were written especially for little people, just like you."

As he spoke, he squeezed his grandchildren and gave them each a tickle, making them giggle and squirm with delight.

"Perhaps you'd like to hear the story of *Greta?*" asked Grandpa, "Or maybe *Martha?* Oh, how about *Frederick and Neville?* That's one of my favourites."

Just then, Ricarda reached out and pointed at the list of titles.

"I'd like this one," she said.

Grandpa smiled. His granddaughter was pointing to the story right at the end of the list. It was entitled, *Ricarda and Samuel.*

"Ah, I think that's a very good choice," said Grandpa, turning to the right page. "Are you sitting comfortably, Ricarda?"

"Yes, Grandpa."

"And are you sitting comfortably, Samuel?"

"Yes, Grandpa, I am."

"In that case, I shall begin."

Ricarda and Samuel smiled, then snuggled together into their Grandpa's lap as he put on his glasses, cleared his throat, and began to read from the book.

"It was difficult to pinpoint exactly what it was about going to Grandpa's house that made it so enjoyable. Yet, for both Ricarda and her younger brother, Samuel, whenever they went to visit him, life just seemed to feel a bit more ... well, special...."

Other books by Richard Storry

The Cryptic Lines

Living as a recluse in his remote gothic mansion, the elderly Lord Willoughby knows that he does not have long to live. With little time remaining, he needs to decide what will become of his vast fortune after his death.

Not content to simply hand everything over to his wastrel son, Matthew, he decides, instead, to set a series of enigmatic puzzles which the son must solve if he is to inherit the estate. However, it emerges that Matthew is not the only interested party. The old house holds many secrets, and nothing is as it first appears....

The Enigma of Heston Grange
The Sequel to The Cryptic Lines

"With the thunder and lightning outside increasing in ferocity, Charles read and re-read the words. Like his name on the envelope, the words of the message within had also been typed – this communication contained no actual handwriting whatsoever. At length, Charles allowed his hand to fall to his lap, the message still held between his fingers. Had there been anyone else present in the room, the words would now have been visible to all. The message read: We know your secret."

What enigma is concealed within the darkened halls of Heston Grange?

And where, exactly, is it hidden?

Order of Merit

In *Order of Merit* we encounter a concert guitarist who is known and loved by audiences all over the world, not only because of his masterful technical skill and compelling musicality, but also because of his charismatic stage personality.

However, his consummate showmanship is merely a cover for his more sinister occupation.

Away from the spotlight he is also a professional hitman – cold, ruthless and efficient. Cunning and calculating, his missions are always accomplished fully, expertly and without a hitch.

But when his next target turns out to be a relative of one of his best friends, things can only get ugly.

The Virtual Lives of Godfrey Plunkett

To relieve his monotonous life of humdrum tedium, Godfrey Plunkett frequently escapes into the world of his fertile imagination. There, away from all criticism and the disparaging looks from his fellow human beings, he can be free to live his dreams. Here, he can be a hero, a celebrity, a movie star – anything he wants.

And, somehow, these inner thoughts help him to maintain his optimism that something fantastic is waiting for him, just around the corner, and is about to happen for real, at any moment.

But, out there in the harsh, real world, will anything fulfilling or exciting ever really happen for this poor, misunderstood individual? Or is he destined to only ever experience the excitement of life within the privacy of his own thoughts?

And, more importantly, what happens when the dividing line between reality and his make-believe world starts to blur?

Come and find out. Come and experience the virtual lives of Godfrey Plunkett.

Ruritanian Rogues, Volume I: A Looming of Vultures

While an ugly war with its neighbouring realm continues to rage, the insulated members of Ruritania's upper classes laugh and dance their way through their superficial lives. Some people, increasingly disillusioned by the pointless conflict, start to consider how the King might be persuaded – or forced – to end it. Meanwhile, an increasing number of items of great value are going missing from those attending these high society gatherings. At whom will the finger of suspicion point? Can anyone be trusted? Why is Captain Golovkin acting so strangely? And is Baron Rudolph really the darling of society he appears to be? In this swirling cauldron of agendas, what will emerge from this looming of vultures?

The Black Talisman

1673: Deep in a deserted forest, a coven of witches is taken by surprise as they attempt to summon the dark Lord, Anubin, from the spirit world.

1984: At his Easter camp, a young boy has an amazing divine encounter. However, as the subsequent years pass, he and his girlfriend find themselves increasingly the subject of demonic visitations.

What is the connection between these seemingly isolated events, over 300 years apart? As the angelic forces of good and evil clash, the mystery gradually emerges.

Can the dark servants of Anubin be prevented from obtaining for him the power he so fervently seeks – the power that comes from the black talisman?

All titles are available from www.crypticpublications.com in paperback, in audio format and as downloads for e-readers.

You can also use this site to contact Richard directly, if you wish. He is always pleased to hear from readers, and will be happy to answer any questions about his books.

Printed in Great Britain
by Amazon